STRANGER IN THE LAND

There wasn't anything about gun fighting that Rig Lashner didn't know. He liked killing. Most of all, Rig Lashner wasn't afraid of death. The chance that he might die never made him nervous. Derek Langston had been a soldier all his life but never a gun fighter. He hired Rig Lashner to teach him because he knew he'd have to fight for his rights and life sooner or later. 'If the day ever comes when I can match you,' Langston said, 'I'll give you a hundred-dollar bonus.' The killer's smile was thin. 'If you ever get to the point where I think you might,' he said, 'I'll make you prove it. You can bet your life on that.'

STRANGER IN THE LAND

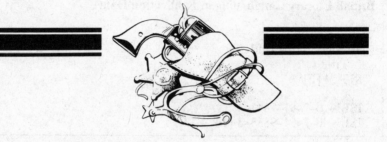

Colby Wolford

ATLANTIC LARGE PRINT
Chivers Press, Bath, England.
Curley Publishing, Inc.,
South Yarmouth, Mass., USA.

Library of Congress Cataloging-in-Publication Data

Wolford, Colby.
   Stranger in the land / Colby Wolford.
     p. cm. (Atlantic large print)
   ISBN 0–7927–0274–3 (soft : lg. print)
   1. Large type books.   I. Title.
[PS3573.05614S7   1990]
813′.54—dc20   90–32694
                                       CIP

British Library Cataloguing in Publication Data

Wolford, Colby
   Stranger in the land.
   I. Title
   813.54 [F]

   ISBN 0–7451–9841–4
   ISBN 0–7451–9853–8 pbk

This Large Print edition is published by Chivers Press, England, and Curley Publishing, Inc, U.S.A. 1990

Published by arrangement with Donald MacCampbell, Inc

U.K. Hardback ISBN 0 7451 9841 4
U.K. Softback ISBN 0 7451 9853 8
U.S.A. Softback ISBN 0 7927 0274 3

FOR ADDIE

CHAPTER ONE

It had been more than a week since the morning in San Antonio when Derek Langston had piled his belongings on the bone-jarring freight wagon and heard the teamster drawl, 'You'll be traveling over a stretch of country that don't never come to an end, and ain't fit to live in—'cept for coyotes and badgers and longhorns and such. And once you hit La Partida, it'll be hard to tell which way is out.'

Now, as the mules slowed near the head of the dusty street that split the squalid little town down the middle, Derek strained his eyes to take in every detail.

They'd said that La Partida was more than a way station; once it had marked the only dependable waterhole for miles in any direction, and gradually its population had swelled to more than a hundred people. But growth had only brought added ugliness, he thought. Sagging frame buildings grayed by the sun and blackened by rain, might mean civilization to the people who lived here; but it was only a crude frontier to an Englishman, even to one who had spent years in Her Majesty's Light Cavalry, and had fought in the chilling blizzards of the Crimea and sweltered in the teeming lands of India.

1

The wagon stopped and Derek pushed back the high-crowned, broad-brimmed Stetson he'd bought in Santone.

The squint-eyed teamster said, 'Well, mister, here's your town and it won't get no prettier as time goes on. You go about your business and I'll dump ever'thing at the hotel like you wanted.'

Derek climbed down and rested one hand on the wagon brake and the other on a mule's rump. 'I'd appreciate that,' he said and realized with a start that his words were not as clipped as they had been a bare few weeks ago. Was it the country that made a man's speech grow softer and slower? He couldn't be sure and didn't know why it made him uncomfortable to think about it.

He lifted his carpetbag from beside the teamster's feet. 'If you need me for anything, I'll be at the bank for the next few minutes.' He eyed the faded sign over the building across the street and added, 'If it still is a bank!'

'It's a bank all right, mister.' The man hesitated, the reins loose in his big callused hands. He said finally, 'I've been hintin' around at somethin' for the last three days, but I've hated to come right out an' say it.'

'I gathered that I wouldn't have an easy time of it, if that's what you mean.'

'Nope, that wouldn't be puttin' it plain enough. The way I see it, you figger all you've

2

got to do is to gather up the longhorns on some ranch you got God-knows-how, then drive 'em up north and pick up your money. You think it's hard work an' that's the end of it, but I'll tell you somethin'. If you drive them cattle out of here before the end of April, you'll likely lose ever' head to the bad weather. And if you try to hold off till then, you won't even be here. The people'll run you out before April, mister.'

Derek stared up at him. 'Why would the people want to run me out?'

'Because they'll want the cattle and you'll be in the way.'

Derek slowly shook his head. 'I came here for a reason. I'll leave the first minute I can, but I'll stay till I've finished.'

The teamster shrugged in defeat. 'Well, I'll give you this much. You don't have to worry about no cattle drive. If you're man enough to stay here and round up a herd, then drive it, say forty miles, till you're clear of La Partida, you'll make it the rest of the way. I'd bet on that.'

Derek stepped back to clear the wagon. 'I have to be man enough.'

'Just the same'—the teamster rubbed the stubble on his broad chin with the palm of his hand—'I'll be back through here in maybe two weeks, and I'll save room for you.' He flipped the curling ribbons of leather. 'Good luck!' The wagon rattled forward, its wheels

3

churning up little spurts of thick white dust.

Derek slapped some of the powdery silt from his worn tweeds and started across the street, a tall man, thirtyish and lean, with a military straightness. The midmorning sun beat down against his back and he unbuttoned the top of his coat. The weather here would take some getting used to; February was supposed to be a cold month, and while dawn had been as chill as an English autumn, it was almost hot now.

As he strode along he looked up and down the street; there were few people to be seen anywhere, but he knew from his experience of the past weeks that shortly there'd be a small crowd of men come to stare at him. Perhaps they came to see what a real stranger, a man from another country, looked like, or perhaps they watched him because of the carpetbag he carried. He'd heard several remarks about the bag already, and all it seemed to symbolize. Had he been able to, he'd have replaced it, but there'd been no time that morning in San Antonio, and no further chance along the way.

There. There was the first man already, stepping out from a small building a hundred yards down the boardwalk. What did they think when they looked at him? That he was stern, a little too concerned with discipline and formality? His soldiers had sometimes gotten that impression at first. It was a result

4

of some peculiar combination of a lean face and thick, sun-bleached eyebrows over a jutting nose that emphasized his darker mustache; maybe even some habitual expression in his blue eyes. No matter. A man wanted to be liked, but he couldn't assume a false look on his face simply because it might please other people.

He rounded the long hitchrail and went to the open door of the ramshackle bank. A myopic, paunchy man was seated behind a desk shoved so near the door that it barely allowed standing room for anyone who entered. Beyond the desk, a black curtain shielded what Derek sincerely hoped would be a safe.

He plopped his carpetbag on the desk and the banker leaned forward with sudden interest, his eyes sharp behind steel-rimmed glasses that sagged halfway down his nose. He reminded Derek of a caricature of Ben Franklin he'd once seen in a London newspaper.

'Yes, sir! Name's Toby Willetts.' He extended a pudgy hand. 'Owner, manager and whatever of the La Partida Bank.'

Derek took the hand. 'Derek Langston—'

Willetts hastened on, 'Haven't lost a nickel now in nigh onto six years. You fixin' to put some money in?'

In answer Derek unstrapped the bag, rummaged in the bottom, and produced a small leather case. He took a sheaf of bills from it and placed it on the desk. 'One thousand dollars. I'll expect to be able to draw any of it, or all of it, whenever I choose.'

Willetts' hand quickly closed on the money and he put it in his lap. Two curious onlookers had already come up behind Derek and were peering through the doorway over his shoulder. Several more were tramping down the boardwalk toward them.

'Yes, sir!' Willetts dug a piece of paper and a pen from one of the drawers, fished at the inkwell on his desk and scratched rapidly over the paper. He slid it forward. 'Here's your receipt. Now mind you don't lose it! Some other feller comes in here with it I'd be bound to give him the money.'

'I'll be careful,' Derek promised. He folded the paper and tucked it in the case. 'Now perhaps you can give me some information. I'd like to get directions to the Tower Ranch.'

'The Tower?' Willetts echoed. He ran a finger behind the glasses and wiped away a speck of matter. 'Well, it ain't hardly what you'd call a ranch no more. What's your interest in it?'

'I own it.'

Willetts' eyes blinked and his finger dug again at the corner of his eye. 'Well, now, Mr. Langston, I'll tell you the truth—I'm glad you're puttin' money in an' not tryin' to

6

borrer. But I don't want to get mixed up in nothin' nor take no sides.'

Derek wet his lips. 'What do you mean by that? The Tower Ranch was purchased from a British corporation. I can prove that, and I'm sure your own county records will prove they owned it.'

Willetts hesitated. 'Like I said, I don't want to take no sides but we've had us a war and the Yankees burned that courthouse down three years ago. Now I ain't sayin' there's no records up in Austin—but I'm sayin' there ain't no records closer'n that.'

'What else are you trying to say?'

Willetts got up with a great creaking of wood. 'You here to look at the ranch or to settle on it?'

'Neither. My primary interest is to gather up the cattle—at least some of them—and take them to market. I've been told it's not safe to leave before the end of April. I can't wait longer than that.'

Willetts patted his arm and looked at him earnestly. 'Look here, son, you figgerin' on buyin' a few supplies and things before you go on out there?'

Derek nodded.

'Then I reckon you can find out just about anything you need to know from Casper Hees. He's the storekeeper, and he'll prob'ly be the mayor if we ever get around to holdin' elections again.' The fat little banker shook

7

his head with a sigh. 'But I got to warn you 'bout one thing—or maybe even more'n one thing. To start with, you bein' a furriner and all, Casper ain't goin' to like it, and a lot of other people'—he nodded toward the men just outside the door—'think just like he wants 'em to. And somethin' else is that bag you're carryin'. We lost that war I was tellin' you about and the Yankees won it and they're tryin' to make us pay for it, and it seems that just about ever' damn one of 'em that comes into this part of the country's got a little carpetbag, just like the one you got. If I was you, I'd put it away somewheres and I wouldn't get it out again until I left—'

Derek laughed. 'I appreciate your interest, but—'

'An' somethin' else,' Willetts added hurriedly. 'Most of the folks around here wear a gun, and there's a good reason for it.'

Derek strapped up the bag and took it from the desk. 'You've been enormously helpful, Mr. Willetts. Thank you. I'll go see this Mr. Hees now.'

He turned around, said, 'Pardon me,' to the seven or eight men jamming the doorway and went out.

He started down the boardwalk, then turned abruptly, almost bumping into a tall, gawky man dressed in the shabby remains of a gray uniform. His face, long and bristled, was not unfriendly, and Derek said, 'I assume

8

you heard what Mr. Willetts said about the store. Could you direct me to Mr. Hees?'

The face split sidewise into a wide grin, showing long yellow teeth. 'Well, now, I reckon if you just go straight ahead about three doors and then turn right, you'd be inside that there store. If you get lost 'tween here and there you just holler and I'll come he'p out.' The men behind him burst out laughing, not entirely at the ex-soldier's wit, Derek realized; some of it was at the stranger's stupidity. But he murmured, 'Thank you,' walked the few steps and entered the store.

Casper Hees was behind the counter, short, stocky and entirely bald except for a narrow horseshoe fringe which circled the long path from temple to temple. His eyes traveled over Derek and he moved around the counter, wiping his hands on his apron. 'Saw you comin' in a while ago,' he said acidly. 'What you want?'

As Derek looked down at the top of Hees's bald head, a fly lit almost exactly in the center of the shiny pate and Hees was forced to slap at it. He glowered, as though feeling a loss of dignity.

Derek moved up to stand in front of him. 'I'll need two things. Supplies and information.' The store smelled of anise and licorice and gingham and gunpowder, of groceries and leather and moldy clothes. He

9

glanced at the crowded merchandise. Hardware spilled over the dry goods and feed elbowed flour. Cans and cases were piled helter-skelter and open barrels crowded the floor. Behind the counter a few guns, both used and new, were prominently displayed for sale. But no chairs huddled around the pot-bellied stove, and one thing Derek had learned already: this was a sure sign that Hees did not welcome casual visitors.

Hees said shortly, 'What kind of information?'

The men were noisily crowding into the store behind Derek now, and he was forced to move to the counter to find enough elbow room to open his bag. He dug inside and pulled out a rolled paper which he spread out on the counter. Hees bustled over and looked at it with interest as Derek slid a finger along the precise, carefully drawn lines. 'This represents La Partida,' he said. 'And this is the headquarters of the Tower Ranch, and this heavier line shows the ranch boundary.'

Hees chuckled gleefully. 'Not no more, it don't!'

Derek studied the man's thick, hard lips. 'What do you mean by that?'

Hees ran his hand roughly across the map. 'All this land in here—the Strip, we call it—belongs to the Judsons now. Delphine Judson, being as how she's the only survivor.'

Derek's eyes moved back to the map. 'And

10

how did she come to get it?'

'She took it, that's how!'

'Then she'll have to give it back. I have deed to it.'

Hees laughed. 'Time you get it back through the courts in maybe five years, there won't be a longhorn in forty miles of it and it'll cost you more'n the land by itself is worth. And maybe you wouldn't ever get it back. 'Sides, you cain't even hold the rest of it, forgettin' about the Strip.'

Derek regarded him curiously, wondering at the unreasoning hatred in his eyes. 'You seem to be uncommonly interested in my success or failure,' he said. 'You don't know anything about me.'

'I don't have to.' Hees hooked his thumbs in his belt. 'I was a member of the Know-Nothin' party and we knew all about furriners. And you're a furriner and a carpetbagger both—and a furrin carpetbagger's worse'n a blue-bellied Yankee carpetbagger, and we don't want your kind in these parts and I figger we won't have you very long.'

Derek brushed the map flat with the palm of his hand. 'Whether you like it or not, I own the Tower Ranch and I'll need directions to get to it. Do you want to give me the information or not?'

Hees said quickly, 'You say you was fixin' to buy supplies?'

11

'Yes. I have a list already made up. But I won't need everything right away. I'll want to ride out for a look before I bother with a wagon.'

Hees looked at him slyly. 'Tell you what, you point out what you want right now. Pay me for all of it and for the rent of a wagon, and I'll have ever'thing loaded up when you get back.'

Someone snickered and Hees flashed him a warning glance, then bent over the map. 'There's a kind of rut runs right from town here, goin' south. May be mostly growed over now—I don't know. You foller that long enough and you'll get there.' His voice grated. ''Thout you get lost and left for the coyotes—and I hope you do!'

Derek was a long time answering, but at last he shrugged. Losing his temper now would make him as ridiculous as the storekeeper. 'All right then.' He pulled a paper from his hip pocket and spread it on the counter. 'You total it up now. I'll pay you and pick up the loaded wagon in less than a week.'

Hees took the list and ran over it with a pencil, elaborately crossing out several items. 'This ain't Philadelphy or Atlanty! This here's a frontier.' He began to put prices alongside the items. Two of these he erased and replaced with higher figures. At length he totaled the long column and the sum was about double what Derek had estimated.

Derek ran the ball of his thumb across his small mustache and thought about it several seconds, then opened his wallet and placed the money on the counter. Hees grabbed at it greedily, wet his thumb and began to count.

'Is there a bootmaker in this town?'

Hees, still counting, was annoyed at the interruption but he nodded. 'Down at the end of the street. Name's Woodruff.'

Derek replaced his wallet and looked down at the hard, shiny pate. 'Then there's just one more thing—about this Know-Nothing party. I never heard of it before but judging from its name I'd say you were an ideal candidate.'

The humorist who had given Derek directions to the store burst out laughing. 'For a carpetbagger,' he roared, 'that's a pretty hot one! An' you want to know somethin'? That's just about what ol' Hees is hisself, if you're willin' to stretch a point or two. He's what you might call a Confed'rate carpetbagger. He stayed home and got rich off'n our wives and young'uns while we was off fightin' the war.'

There was a shuffle of feet from the other men but no echoing mirth. Hees spun savagely around. 'Let me tell you somethin', Otis! I ain't been gettin' rich lately off your wife and young'un. You know why? 'Cause you owe me groceries for two months, that's why!'

Otis' face fell and he, too, shuffled his feet. 'Aw, now, Casper, wait a minute. You know I didn't mean nothin'.'

'You think you're a real stud, don't you?' Hees asked. He lifted his thick, muscular arms. 'Well, let me tell you somethin' else—in my day I've made men like you crawl on their bellies. Now you come over here. After this furriner leaves I want to talk to you 'bout settlin' up this here bill.'

Otis snorted. 'Aw, hell, Casper—'

'You do like I say!'

Derek replaced the papers in his carpetbag, fastened it and started out. He carefully threaded his way through the crowd, half of whom sported at least a week's growth of beard. When he reached the walk somebody close behind him said, 'We goin' to foller him?'

'Naw, hell, not for a minute. Let's see what old Hees's got to say.'

Derek moved on to the corner, glad of the moment's respite. It seemed as though everyone minded a stranger's business in this country; he had steeled himself to ignore it, but he couldn't pretend he liked it.

The small saddle shop and boot store reeked of tanned leather and he took a good long whiff of it. It was the smell of an old familiar friend and he stood for a moment savoring it, then crossed to the counter where a solemn, skinny little man was stitching a

14

saddle bag. He looked up, his face lined with ten thousand wrinkles. 'What can I do for you?'

'I'd like to see a pair of boots.'

Woodruff put down his needle, dug behind the short counter and pulled up a boot. 'One like this'n here?'

'That wasn't quite what I had in mind. Something with heavier heels and not quite so blunt across the toes.'

He replaced it and dug up another. 'Like this'n, then?'

Derek shook his head. 'Not that, either.' He looked down at his own boots. They were comfortable, but they'd been made to be worn with jodhpurs instead of breeches and they were intended to hold small, light cavalry spurs and gleam against the background of an English army saddle. They'd be almost worthless in this country. He turned at the tramp of feet on the boardwalk. Hees must have finished, for the crowd that had dogged him was coming to the door of the shop now, led by Otis.

Derek looked down at Otis' boots. They were run over and worn through, but once they'd had slick, shiny tops and smooth lowers, with medium high heels. 'I'll have a pair like he's wearing,' he said.

Otis stood in the door, hitching his pants, a look of burning anger on his face. 'Maybe you'd just like to take these, Mister

Greenhorn.'

Derek quickly looked past Otis and examined the faces of the other men, trying to determine if he had offended Otis and should apologize or if this were Hees's doing.

The rest of them were nudging each other and watching gleefully; if Otis had been offended they'd surely have been angry along with him. But there was still a chance that he'd actually hurt the man's feelings.

'I meant no offense,' he said.

Otis' voice was savage. 'You don't have to mean no offense. I feel the same way Hees does about a furrin carpetbagger, on'y I'm fixin' to do somethin' about it.' He took off his gunbelt and handed it to someone in the crowd. 'You're lucky you ain't wearin' a gun, mister, but bein's you ain't, you just step out here and take your beatin' like a man—if you are a man.'

Derek's eyes narrowed. There was no way out, and he knew it as well as every man there. No matter what he'd said, Otis would have picked it up.

Woodruff said quickly, 'Not in the store now. Not in the store!'

Derek made one last attempt. 'I've apologized. That's all I can do.'

Otis stubbornly shook his head. 'It ain't all you can do. Fight's what you can do. You make up your mind now—in or out. I'm tired waitin'.'

'Not in the store!' the wrinkled bootmaker insisted, and dragged up a heavy six-gun and set it on the counter. 'As a customer, mister, you're welcome,' he said. 'But right now you better get out of here.'

Derek looked at Otis' hardened face with a sense of disbelief; he'd known there would be violence in this land, had expected it. An argument, perhaps—hot words over disputed land or cattle, leading to a fight that couldn't be avoided. But he hadn't been prepared for this—a cold, ruthless, pointless fight, simply because he hadn't been born here. Right here in Southern territory; it wouldn't even have helped if he'd been born in the northern United States.

He put his hat on the counter, slid out of his jacket, and moved slowly to the door. Otis backed away to let him pass, but the moment his foot touched the boardwalk the man swung. Derek cocked his head to the right and the bruising knuckles slid up the side of his temple. The stinging blow seemed to have pulled all the hair from that side of his head, but it had left Otis off balance. Derek quickly stomped the toe of the worn boot and as Otis howled, he grabbed the man's hair in his left hand and brought the heel of his right fist against his jaw in a savage hammerlike blow. Otis rocked back against the wall and the building shook. A shocked look passed over his face, but he was no coward. His mouth

17

turned down at the corners and he pushed himself from the wall, swinging with the other hand.

Derek stepped inside to block the blow and it was a mistake. Otis weighed well over two hundred pounds and the thirty-pound weight advantage, combined with the enormous strength in his arms, was too much. The inside of his arm thudded against Derek's shoulder and sent him crashing against the doorjamb.

Derek was away with a quick rebound. He lashed a left into Otis' belly and followed with a right to his mouth; then a heavy bruising fist caught him squarely in the forehead. He went down and rolled as some of the crowd yelled, 'Boot him, Otis! Boot him!' Instead, Otis dived full-length on top of his rolling body. The air spurted from Derek's lungs leaving him weak and numb.

Otis grabbed his hair and slammed his head against the boardwalk in a rapid tattoo. Yellow fire flashed in his brain and turned to bright red. He gasped for air, felt it start to filter back into his lungs. His strength began to return in spite of the dizziness. But Otis felt the growing threat. He shifted his left hand to Derek's hair and began to pummel his face with a bruising right.

The blows stopped stinging and an alarm rang in Derek's mind. When he could no longer feel he would be unconscious and he was fighting a stranger, surrounded by a crowd of angry strangers. If he couldn't handle the one man then he'd never be able to handle the crowd; he'd be beaten before he started.

His groping hand slid upward and found Otis' mouth. A forefinger slid between Otis' teeth and his upper lip and Derek pushed. Otis groaned and the hammer blows stopped.

A steely hand encircled Derek's wrist. He had the presence of mind to close his fist quickly to keep his finger from being bitten off; then somehow he realized that Otis was sitting on top of him, with his leg bent so that his left foot was near Derek's right hand. He caught the booted toes and twisted, and at the same time rolled.

Otis was slammed to his side and Derek pushed himself free. He scrambled to his feet and staggered backward several steps, unable to keep his balance. A rough shove sent him hurtling forward again into Otis, who was just rising to his feet. His head began to clear, but a burning rage dimmed his thinking more than Otis' savage blows. The attack had been needless and ruthless but, by God, he'd been in fights before—with slashing steel and flailing chain as well as savage knuckles.

He lowered his head and swung short jarring blows to Otis' midsection. The hammer blows about his own head ceased to rain so heavily. He continued to swing and

19

Otis' arms lowered to defend his belly.

Derek opened his fist and swung with all the weight of his body. The edge of his palm caught Otis just over the jugular vein and he sank to the boardwalk, groaning. His eyes were glazed and his mouth opened. Blood from a split inner lip trickled from the corner of his mouth and dripped down his chin.

Derek staggered back against the wall and faced the crowd, his lungs screaming for air. Casper Hees shouldered his way through and stood in front of him, and Derek found enough breath to say, 'If another man—touches me, now or later—I'll assume you put him up to it—and you'll pay—blow for blow!'

With cold fury, Hees said, 'Why don't you get back on that wagon and get out of here? You're nothin' but a furriner! We got our rules here, and our ways of doin' things! And you don't fit in, mister!'

Derek pushed himself forward and Hees backed away, his lips twisting. 'You won't last a week! You better save your hide while you can!'

Derek stood panting and his eyes traveled slowly upward. Sometime during the fight a group of riders had ridden up close and were now sitting their horses, watching. The nearest was a girl, though she was dressed as roughly as the others. Beneath the flat-crowned black hat and the tumbled black

20

curls, he saw a face which would have been beautiful but for the cold light in her hard gray eyes, and the tight smile that lifted the corners of her wide mouth.

He raised his hand and rubbed it down the side of a bloody temple. He'd seen hard women before, but somehow, when a man was bleeding, they became soft and feminine and compassionate, and they set about patching him up. But this one seemed only to be losing interest because now the fight was over. They were all hard, he thought, every damned bloody son of them, and the women, too.

He wiped the blood off his hand with a handkerchief. He daubed his temple, then held the bloody cloth up toward the girl. 'You can take this home with you, if you like to look at blood,' he offered.

The girl laughed; but when she spoke, the amusement in her husky voice was tempered with sharpness. 'If I need any blood, I'll draw it myself!'

He turned away, pocketing the handkerchief. Hees moved alongside him, his lips still twisted. 'You ain't fought nobody yet! Otis is just a town loafer. That there's Delphine Judson. It's her that's got the Strip.'

'Then I'll discuss it with her when I'm ready to talk about it.' The boardwalk cleared in front of Derek and he moved on toward the hotel.

'You got me all wrong,' Hees called. 'I didn't say I was turnin' you over to her. I ain't through yet—not by a damn sight!'

CHAPTER TWO

As he neared the livery stable Derek spat on the edge of the dusty street. Lunch at the hotel had left a bad taste in his mouth, but he could say one thing in favor of this country—if you wanted to spit you didn't have to stop to consider—you spat.

He went through the open doors of the stable, and the thickset old hostler limped forward from the dark shadows to meet him, using a pitchfork for a cane. 'All set,' he nodded. 'Horse is saddled and your gear's aboard. Mind you treat that horse good!'

Derek was examining the saddled horse when he heard shuffling footsteps nearing the stable door. He looked over his shoulder in time to see Otis pass by, head down. On a sudden impulse he called sharply, 'Mr. Otis!'

Otis stopped and looked blankly behind him; then as Derek came into the bright sunlight he turned defensively. His long face wore a hangdog look, but his fists doubled with determination.

Derek drew up to him and shook his head

22

slightly. 'I didn't call you back to fight again. Do you know anything about cattle?'

Otis looked at him suspiciously. 'Some. I was raised on a farm and last year I was on two cattle drives—far as they went.'

'Good enough,' Derek nodded. 'Do you own a horse?'

'Yeah, I got a good horse.' His eyes lit with hope. 'Do you mean—after—' He stopped short, looking at Derek's puffed face.

'I'm not trying to shake hands and be friends, if that's what you mean,' Derek said coldly. 'But I do need somebody to work for me. I'll pay you thirty dollars a month.'

Otis' hangdog expression was gone; he looked as though he might jump up and down with joy, but a cloud quickly passed over his face. 'There's only one thing, mister. I cain't go off out of town like this and leave my wife without no money a-tall. Not with Hees madder'n a skinned 'coon 'cause I got whipped. If I could have just three or four dollars it'd be enough to tide her over.'

Derek pulled out his wallet, extracted thirty dollars and thrust it out. 'Your first month's wages. I'll expect you back here saddled and ready to go in fifteen minutes.'

Otis grabbed the money. 'I'll be here,' he said. 'Don't you worry none about that.' He took off, rapidly angling across the street. He was trotting before he reached the corner.

Derek went back into the stable. The

hostler, leaning on the pitchfork, turned heavily to follow his movements as he walked over to a small enclosure and examined four unsaddled horses. His eyes settled with satisfaction on a zebra-striped dun gelding. 'You can unsaddle that mustang,' he said. 'I'll take the dun.'

'Now wait a minute,' the hostler protested. He hobbled forward. 'That dun ain't for hire. That's my personal horse.'

'How often do you ride him?'

The hostler stopped, blinking. 'Why, I reckon I don't, much.'

'Then he must need some exercise. I'll be gone less than a week and I'll take good care of him.'

'Well, now—' The hostler scratched his head. 'Well, now—you might have a point there. The only thing is, there's some think you might not come back.'

'I'll be back,' Derek said, 'in less than a week. And I'll be here as long after that as I think necessary.'

'Well, now—seein' what you done to Otis, and seein's how you turned right around and hired him, maybe I'll take a chance. An' I'll give you credit for one thing—you know horseflesh.' He reached into his pocket for a twist of tobacco, bit off a healthy chew, and started to unloose the saddlebags. 'You set a spell whilst I change the gear.'

Derek said, 'Thanks,' and nodded slightly.

He looked about the stable, then went over to the doorjamb and stood in the edge of the sunlight, glancing out over the little town. It was a derelict town, he thought, in derelict country, and he should have felt some kinship with it, because he was as much a derelict as any of it. He thought of Hees's words, *You don't fit in, mister*! Why did that antagonize him? he wondered. Who in hell wanted to fit in here?

The clop-clop of Otis' bay horse broke his reverie. As the man reined up close Derek saw that his saddle was scarred and cracked and even his bedroll was ragged; but there was nothing worn and battered about the .44 Colt revolver at his waist. Derek pushed his Stetson back and squinted up at him. There'd been a change in the set of the man's face, he thought. The hangdog look was gone. But there was a tinge of uneasiness in its place. He probably wanted to apologize for the fight and Derek decided to let him squirm a bit. 'Do you know how to get to the Tower Ranch, Mr. Otis?'

Otis nodded. 'Yeah. I was there oncet. I know the way all right.' He glanced behind Derek. 'Harlan's got your horse ready.'

The hostler said, as he led out the dun, 'Now mind you take good care of him!'

'I will,' Derek said and swung into the saddle gently urging the horse to his left. The saddle would take some getting used to; it bore far more resemblance to a medieval Spanish war rig than to the modern English army saddle, but he'd be willing to bet that he'd rarely ridden a better horse.

They moved off and as they passed Hees's place, the storekeeper came out and stood in the doorway glowering.

'Maybe it's a good thing you've got that thirty dollars,' Derek said. 'I don't think your credit's much good any more.'

'When my wife pays old Hees tomorrer mornin',' Otis said grimly, 'it'll be the first time we been clear out of debt to him since the spring of '62 when I rode off to war. And don't think he didn't keep me over the coals for it.' He grinned. 'The next time I see him he better give me a good smile or I'll bust his teeth.'

They rode south out of town and cut onto what once might have been a trail, and the land rolled and twisted in front of them with no sign of human habitation as far as the eye could see. Derek began slowly to let his mind relax, to look at the surrounding country, to feel the vast distances. He slowed the dun to a walk so he could see it all more clearly: the gully-laced brown land beginning to show a touch of green; the profusion of mesquite trees no higher than a mounted man's head; the wide flats where the only sound above the steady thud of horses' hoofs and the rebellious squeak of hard leather was the

26

scurrying of rats at the dead bases of shoulder-high prickly pear bushes. He lifted his head. The air was filled with the tangy smell of stubborn plants gathering strength to shoot out green leaves in the forthcoming spring, and to defend themselves from the summer heat which would follow.

They rode through a strip of stiff-limbed blackjack brush, and then over a low hill, dotted with rust-colored rocks. At the bottom of the hill Otis pulled his horse even with Derek's and blurted out the thing he had been wanting to say.

'Mister, I might as well tell you somethin'—what I mean is—I don't want you to figger you're gettin' somethin' and then not gettin' it.'

When Derek didn't answer he hurried on, as though afraid of losing his nerve.

'What I'm tryin' to say is, I done an awful thing in '62. I went off to war and left my wife and kids—left 'em to starve just about.' He looked at Derek almost defiantly. 'Me, all fired up to be a big hero and not thinkin' 'bout nobody else! Mister, I'll tell you somethin'—I had two kids when I left and one when I come back. An' my wife looked twenty years older—an' I wasn't gone but three years.' He was speaking now with intensity of feeling that was almost embarrassing. 'She suffered, that woman did, an' I aim to make it up to her somehow.' He

27

gulped, groping for words, shaken at his inability to express himself.

'What I'm tryin' to say is, I'll work—and I'll work hard. Any kind of job you want me to do. But if it comes to fightin', mister, then I've had my fill of it. An' it's goin' to come to it and we both know it, and I ain't leavin' no widder just for the sake of thirty dollars a month. You want me to settle up and go back?'

Derek eyed him sharply. 'You seemed willing enough to fight this afternoon.'

Otis squirmed. 'That was different. You wasn't wearin' no gun. But you won't see nobody else not wearin' one around here, and there's plenty knows how to use 'em, too.' He shifted his own gun and his voice took on a pleading quality. 'Look, I mentioned about me bein' on two cattle drives last year—well, it was guns kep' us from gettin' there both times. They was Delphine Judson's herds and she's a fightin' woman and she come back an' rounded up another herd an' the third time she made it. But I wasn't along. An' you know why? Because it just plumb didn't make sense for me to go out and get killed, that's why. Seein' how I felt she didn't even ask me to go. All she took was the tough ones that didn't mind killin', or gettin' shot at, and they're the ones workin' for her now.'

Derek thoughtfully slid his fingers through the dun's mane. 'We'll worry about fighting if

28

it comes to that,' he said. 'I'm not here to fight. I'm here to get a herd of cattle to an eastern market.'

'Then it's all settled about me not fightin'?'

'It's all settled,' Derek said gravely. Wars did different things to different people, he reflected. Some men spent all their lives reliving their military careers; some refused to give up their guns and went looking for other wars to fight, like the men working for Miss Judson; and some, because of the things they'd seen and the deeds they'd done, hoped to God they'd never see action again. Otis was like that; he wondered briefly under which heading he himself fit, then wrenched his mind back and away.

'What lies south of the Tower Ranch?' he asked.

'South? Nothin'. Nothin' a-tall. Some say it's part of a Spanish land grant, reco'nized by the courts. But there ain't nobody out there, less'n it's a band or two of Comanches and Kiowas. There's ranches to the east though; but they're on the other side of a big hogback ridge that nobody ever crosses. This land we're on now belongs to the state, and it's bone dry. Ever'thing to the west is Delphine Judson's.'

'Aren't there any farms out here?'

'Some, west of La Partida.'

'Then, if there's so much land, why does Delphine Judson want the Strip?'

29

'It's low land, and it's got water on it most of the year, and the cattle are thickest there.' He shook his head. 'Her pa never would have took somethin' that didn't belong to him, but Delphine figgers different. Nobody could believe what she was like when we come back from the war.'

Derek smiled grimly. 'Maybe you didn't know what she was like before the war.'

'I knew,' Otis said matter-of-factly. 'And so did ever'body else. Her pa raised our cavalry unit, and we was all in it, includin' her two brothers and their foreman, Billy Cedar. Delphine was about seventeen then, as sweet a girl as you could ever find. She rode with us as far as Santone and was supposed to stay with relatives till the war ended. Them days we figgered it'd be done with in no time—one charge and the Yankees'd scatter from hell to Georgia.'

He was quiet and only the steady clop-clop of the horses broke the silence. Then he added softly, 'Her pa and both her brothers got killed at Shiloh two months later. She come back by herself, and she had trouble with the ranch gettin' raided two, three times. Nobody knows what happened that last time, but when the war was over she was diff'rent. Billy Cedar tried to straighten her out, but even he cain't do nothin'. She seems to have forgot that he was once a sort of second pa to her. Now she just keeps him 'cause he knows cattle and can handle men.'

Derek fell to speculating. How did you go about standing up to a woman who claimed your land, and seemed willing to fight for it? If you waited for the courts, it would take too long, far too long. No, she'd have to give up the Strip in the next week or two, and he'd have to find a way to make her do it.

Otis looked over his shoulder at the sinking sun. His head swiveled back and his eyes searched the land in front of them until he spotted a small stand of stunted ebony trees. 'Yonder's as good a place as any to camp,' he said. 'An' you'll need to be fresh when we get there in the mornin'. Likely you're expectin' to find a good-sized ranch house topped by a high lookout tower, but you might's well know now. It was burned in '63 by Comanches or somebody. An' I might's well out with why I was tellin' you about not bein' a fightin' man. We won't be alone when we get there. I hear there's a Yankee and a Mexkin already out there, ready to take over ever' head of stock and ever' foot of land that Delphine Judson ain't already took.'

CHAPTER THREE

Soft breezes rustled the thin leaves of mesquite trees and filtered gently through

31

patches of dry grass. Somewhere far beyond the fading embers of the small campfire, coyotes howled over the lowlands, and the cries swept on and on, filled with sadness. It was a strange sound, but it was stranger still that he was here to listen to it—he, Derek Langston, born during the reign of William the Fourth, two years before Victoria became Queen, and lately an officer in the 11th (Prince Albert's Own) Hussars.

He looked at the softly snoring Otis, feeling some subtle need for companionship, but quickly rejecting it, as was his habit. You couldn't share with other people the things that lay in your mind, he thought. Not most people. Sam Otis, who had lived a different life on a different continent, could never understand the tangle of events which had brought him here.

No, he was being unfair. Much of it was not understandable even to himself. It started with a kind of unquenchable restlessness or feeling of dissatisfaction, or perhaps some half-uncovered sense of rebellion at the thought of conforming to a pattern not of his own making. Whatever it was, it had kept him for years at the lonely outposts, where occasional sharp moments of danger exploded to break the monotony.

And perhaps that made him partly responsible for what his father had done. Maybe if he had not stayed in the army he could have prevented it. Letters from friends back home had told him what was happening; after his mother's death his father had begun to speculate. At first it was only in a small way, and the income from the estates in Northumberland that had been in the family for eight hundred years more than covered it. But as gamble after gamble failed the elder Langston took wilder and more desperate chances, till the land stood mortgaged and the income could be used only to pay interest charges.

They'd both had plenty of precedent, Derek decided. For his own part most of his family had been in the Services at one time or another. They had helped to thwart many an attack on the island, and they'd fought in the Crusades, and in the countless wars against France and Spain—wherever other Englishmen had fought.

And there'd been Langstons like his father who had mortgaged the estates until the financial manipulations of a genius or the right marriage was required to get them untangled again. As long as an entail forbade their sale without the heir's permission, the estates could always be saved somehow.

But his father had shattered precedent by using neither of the accepted and time-honored solutions. Instead, he had sold the land by forging Derek's name to papers breaking the entail.

It was years before Derek, half the world away in India, learned all the details; years in which army life became more and more intolerable. Twice he'd had to refuse promotion because he hadn't the money for the purchase; twice he'd seen younger and less experienced officers assume commands which had first been offered to him. And still his father's glowing letters told only of the bright prospects of this investment, of that speculation.

When the end came, one final speculation was all that remained. The note which explained it had been written two days before his father died.

'The Tower Ranch was never worth much money,' he wrote. 'During the American Civil War it brought in nothing, and last year's cattle drives throughout the state of Texas were less than successful. For these reasons I was able to get the Tower for only two thousand pounds. The rest is up to you. If you're able to market all the wild cattle there, one day you might have enough money to return and redeem what I've lost. But you'll have to make your first drive quickly. One thousand pounds was all I could scrape together. The other thousand is due in July. Imagine—only one thousand pounds left, and I had so much in the beginning! I've been a complete fool...'

It had been too late in the game to hesitate,

and far too late to castigate either himself or his father. The sale of his Captaincy and whatever else he could part with had brought Derek this far—to a race against time, and to a fight against people he'd never known existed. But maybe it would be worth it.

He wondered what the first Langston would think if he could see this land. In a way, one could even say he'd reached across the centuries and bought the Tower Ranch...

Derek rolled over on the hard ground, wrapping the thin blanket tighter around his shoulder. Otis sat up, fumbling for his gun.

'Somethin' wrong, Mr. Langston?'

'No, nothing wrong,' Derek said. 'I was listening to the coyotes and thinking about an ancestor of mine who's been dead for almost eight hundred years. And I was wondering what he'd think. In a way, you might say I inherited this land from him.'

Otis stared wide-eyed for a moment, then shook his head and silently sank back onto his blanket.

★　　★　　★

Breakfast was tough bread, salt bacon and steaming coffee. Afterwards, Otis scoured the cooking utensils while Derek brought up the horses. When the animals were saddled, Otis scratched his jaw and ventured a timid

35

suggestion. 'If I was you, I'd lead that there dun a few steps to take the vinegar out of him.'

Derek nodded as he rubbed the horse's nose. Why should he think that people from other lands were different, he wondered, when horses the world over had so many traits in common?

The air was clean and cold and fresh. Shiny droplets of dew clung to clumps of green grass at the base of the ebony trees, and to a large, beautifully patterned spider web masterfully engineered to encompass a troughlike area between two of the tree limbs. The land was different today, Derek thought. And the sounds were different. Mockingbirds were singing now, occasionally interrupted by the sawlike calls of woodpeckers. Other birds were chirping in the distance; every shrub and bush seemed to be full of them.

They rode into a small clearing and a dozen wild-eyed longhorns bolted in all directions. The sound of their brush-crashing retreat lasted long after they were out of sight.

Otis grinned nervously. 'Them are the gentle ones. We'll see some mean'uns later on.'

*　　*　　*

The Tower ranch house had been built on level ground, but when the tower itself had been standing, its occupants could doubtless have seen for miles in three directions, and perhaps even to the east over the low hill that reared up a quarter mile away. Now all that remained of the house was a fireplace and portions of the four walls, varying in height from three to six feet. Some freak of nature, perhaps a timely rain storm, had spared that much. If so, the log corral—recognizable now only because it was a circle of charred stumps and hard ashes—and the long slim rectangular ruin which once must have been a bunkhouse, had been burned first.

A horse nickered from beyond the remains of the house. Derek's dun threw up its head and answered, but they were within fifty yards of the charred walls before two men, rifles thrust in front of them, moved out through the open doorway. Otis drew a deep, sharp breath. His hand tightened on the reins, but he kept himself from pulling the bay to a stop.

Derek watched the two men as they assumed a posture of careless readiness just outside the doorway. The man on the left was the broader of the two. He was fair-complected, with woolly brown hair thrusting out from beneath a high-crowned, pearl-gray Stetson, and his eyes were rounded so that broad circles of white were visible beyond his hard brown irises. A deep crease projected downward from the base of each nostril to the corners of his mouth. He wore blue duck breeches and jacket and stood with his legs wide apart in purposeful assurance.

His companion was slimmer, swarthy and slightly taller. His low-crowned black hat, embroidered black jacket and tight-fitting black pants which flared at the bottom were the dress of a Mexican of wealth and position—or perhaps one who wished to leave that impression. A slim mustache painted a line above wide lips which smiled easily under an aquiline nose and piercing black eyes. He was by far the handsomer of the two, and his movements were those of a man who would strike swiftly at the first sign of trouble, rather than stand bull-strong and unyielding like the man at his side.

Derek motioned Otis to pull over while he rode directly up to them and dismounted.

The woolly-headed one shot a glance at Derek's hip, quickly raised his eyes in search of armament which might be concealed inside his shirt, then half-swung his rifle toward Otis. His voice carried a deep wheeze in spite of the thickness of his chest and Derek noted a heavy scar at the base of his throat. But his remark was directed at Otis. 'You somebody we ought to know?' he asked.

Otis recoiled. 'Not me! Name's Otis. Sam Otis.'

The man smiled. 'Mine's Joe Griff. And with me here is Miguel Cervantes.' His eyes carried hard amusement as he looked at Derek. 'I didn't figure a man'd be fool enough to ride through this country on a good horse like that and not pack a gun. Not unless he had a gun fighter with him—somebody like Rig Lashner, maybe.'

Derek shook his head and said shortly, 'I've no reason to have a gunfighter with me.'

Griff laughed at his clipped tones. 'An Englishman! No damned wonder.'

He and Cervantes visibly relaxed, but Griff's face quickly clouded over and turned hard. 'What do you want here?' he demanded.

'I'll ask you the same.'

'And I'll tell you quick enough.' His accent was different from the others'; it was harsher, faster. 'Cervantes and me are makin' a cattle drive come spring. We're partners, and we're just startin' out, but we'll have plenty of friends here a month from now. And this is where we're gettin' our cattle.'

Derek felt a chill growing inside him. Not at the men who stood before him with ready guns, but at the anger that throbbed in his own temples. What made him want to swell up and fight when only a month ago he'd have been willing to arbitrate a dispute like this? It was not in his nature to back down, but why didn't he think first of settling the whole thing legally and in an orderly manner?

'I have a legal claim to the land you're

standing on, and to all the cattle on it,' he said.

The wheeze in Griff's voice grew deeper as he patted his rifle and said, 'We've got a claim, too.'

'You can fight, señor, or leave,' Cervantes added.

Derek heard Otis' breath whistle as he said, 'For the moment I'll leave. But it's only because I'm new to this sort of thing, and I'm not sure I know what to do about it.' He pointed to the low hill to his left. 'And I'm only going as far as that hill until I think about it. We'll settle everything when I come back.'

'It is settled already,' Cervantes said softly.

'He's right,' Griff agreed. 'You can ride off and never come back, or we can bury you on that hill.'

Derek swung up onto the dun and Otis said quickly, 'I'll go along.'

'No, you'll stay here!' Derek snapped. 'I'm not running out, if that's what you're afraid of.' He wheeled the dun and touched his boot heels lightly to his flanks.

As he rode off at a gallop, the heel of his clenched fist slid over the wide, flat saddlehorn. It was frustrating and hard to understand that the documents he carried in one of the saddlebags flapping behind him were worthless. Civilization might as well be a million miles away. Everything here belonged not to someone who had a legal claim, but to someone who was strong.

The dun climbed the slope of the hill and Derek pulled him to a halt beside a gnarled mesquite. The horse champed at the bit and he spoke soothingly, 'Steady, boy. Steady now.' The dun quieted, but Derek sat stiff and straight, his lips tightly compressed. A few feet away a cottontail belatedly decided that he was on unsafe ground and bolted off in an erratic zigzag course that crossed the path of a covey of running quail. The quail scattered with a flutter of wings that shook the air.

Derek reached over and gingerly raked his thumb across the point of a mesquite thorn, looking out across the wide expanse of land below him. Small herds of longhorns dotted the landscape and he knew from the things he had learned from the teamster, and from what he'd seen for himself, that deer were out there, too, and coyotes and wolves and havoline hogs, and badgers and armadillos and raccoons and opossums. And there were jack rabbits by the thousands, and wildcats and mountain lions, and wild turkeys, and doves, ducks, geese—whatever a man could think of.

He was aware now that the sun was beating down on him just as it had yesterday at this time, making him uncomfortably warm after the chill cold of the morning. His glance raked across scrub brush, took in the thorny prickly pear and moved over the ground-hugging cactus the teamster had called *pitaya*. This was a lonely, desolate land and most of the creatures in it, and most of the plant life, were armed for conflict.

It was then that something happened to Derek Langston. Perhaps it was some mysterious force in the air that folded about a man and molded him, or perhaps it was something in the soil which rose up to grip his insides and tell him what kind of a man he would be, now that he was here. Whatever it was, it had happened to Englishmen before, and to people from other nations, and it was apt to happen to others in the future.

He slid his hand up between the dun's ears and rubbed gently. 'I know now how he felt,' he said aloud. 'He's been dead for eight hundred years, and I know how he felt that first day, when he sat his horse high on a rocky hill and looked at all that lay below him.'

He reached his hand back to his saddlebag, unfastened the thong and felt inside. The long-barreled Webley revolver he dragged out had been with him for a long time. It was as deadly as any revolver made. He had not intended ever to fire it again except for harmless amusement; but now something had happened. The whole world was different. He thrust it in his belt, wheeled the dun and

42

started back down the slope toward the ranch house.

CHAPTER FOUR

Griff and Cervantes had leaned their rifles against the blackened doorway and were talking to the dismounted Otis, who was fidgeting and glancing back over his shoulder. His relief was evident now as Derek pulled up and swung down in front of them; then simultaneously, all three saw the gun in his belt.

Cervantes recoiled, his right hand instantly hovering over the revolver at his hip; Griff stood stock still. Otis began carefully to edge away.

Derek kept his eyes on the other two, but made a motion toward Otis with his head. 'You get on your horse and ride down the road a way. I'll shout when I want you to come back.'

Otis needed no urging; and as he hit the saddle and swung his horse about, Derek noticed with satisfaction that the maneuver had caught Griff and Cervantes off balance. The Mexican edged slowly to Derek's right, but Griff refused to budge.

'Did you really come back down here to fight us?' he asked incredulously.

'If I have to. You're on my land. You're trying to take what's mine.'

Cervantes' silky voice cut in, 'Then, señor, fight!'

'Wait!' Griff snapped. 'There's somethin' fishy here. You think you can make a belt-draw and beat both of us?'

'Beat you? Maybe you'd shoot first, if that's what you mean.'

'Then how in hell do you figure to win?'

Derek touched the tip of his tongue to the corner of his mouth, cut in yesterday's fight. 'Perhaps I won't,' he said. 'That's what we have to see, isn't it?' He took two steps forward and stood almost touching Griff, and Cervantes' palm slapped the butt of his revolver.

In one continuous movement, Derek shouldered into Griff, grabbed his wrist and spun him around. He tugged at the gun in his belt as they wrestled. The sight hooked and held and he twisted to pull it free, keeping Griff between him and Cervantes.

The Mexican circled like a high-stepping tiger, but Derek managed to keep the struggling Griff between them. Then the Webley was out and jamming into Griff's ribs. Griff flinched, caught himself and stood still, his breath wheezing hoarsely. Cervantes froze.

'That was the God-damnedest fool thing I ever saw,' Griff wheezed. 'You've got no

44

more notion how to fight with a gun than some plowboy that never killed nothin' but rabbits.'

'Tell your friend to put his gun on the ground,' Derek said softly. 'Then perhaps we can talk.'

A burning hard light of refusal came in Cervantes' eyes, but Griff said, 'Mike, put it down! Put it down, Mike! Let's hear what he's got to say.'

Cervantes stood unmoving for a long interval, then slowly let the hammer down, picked a clean, hard spot on the ground and gently placed the gun at his feet.

Derek's left hand slid Griff's gun out of its holster and he backed away and stood against the wall, the Webley held ready. He looked for a moment at the two unarmed, silent men. 'All right,' he said. 'You were going to gather a herd and drive them north. What were you going to use for money?'

'We don't need money,' Griff said scornfully. 'What the hell do we need money for?'

'Can you get a crew who'll work for nothing?'

Griff nodded savagely. 'We can. We've got friends—here and in Mexico. They'll work for nothing and when we reach the end of the trail we'll split the profits.'

'And what will you eat in the meantime? Beef? Don't you need flour, sugar, salt, bacon, gunpowder, balls, caps? Will you ride unshod horses and cut your firewood with belt knives? Suppose your saddletree gets broken, will you ride bareback? And what will you do for a chuck wagon? Will you carry food and bedding both behind your saddle?'

Cervantes stepped forward, the gun at his feet almost forgotten. 'What do you wish to say, señor?'

'Simply this—I have money to hire a crew and buy the supplies we'll need. Work with me instead of the men you were going to send for. Help me organize and conduct a drive and when we get the cattle to market I'll give each of you five per cent. Would you have gotten that much if you'd had to split with your friends?'

Griff and Cervantes seemed to have forgotten Derek's gun as they gave each other a knowing look, and Derek was hard put to hide the satisfaction in his own eyes.

'Maybe he's got something there,' Griff said finally.

'I will do it,' Cervantes announced. 'We are partners. We will trust each other, beginning at once!' He spun around, stooped and retrieved his gun. Derek was almost ready to fire when the revolver slid expertly into the greased holster.

'Yep, we've got a deal,' Griff said and held out his hand for his Colt.

For a split second Derek studied them, the

46

Webley still held ready, the Colt still loose at his side. If that look between them had been what he thought it was, they'd decided in that moment to use him, to use his money, his crews, his supplies—and then to take his cattle. And if that were true they wouldn't do anything now, or tomorrow, or next week; they'd wait till he was no longer of any use to them.

He thrust the Webley through his belt, handed the Colt to Griff and waited.

Cervantes tapped the top of his low-crowned sombrero and stretched his full lips into a gleaming smile. 'There is something I wish to know,' he said slyly. 'You can use the gun?'

Derek nodded sharply. 'I can use it.'

'You will show us?'

'I will show you. But I'd best call Otis first, or he might leave.' He cupped his hands over his mouth and shouted sharply, 'Otis!'

A hundred yards down the wagon road Otis rode his bay out of a stand of brush, stopped and stared solemnly. Apparently satisfied, he urged the bay forward and galloped up to them.

'There's going to be some shooting,' Derek said shortly, 'and I didn't want you to get the wrong impression. Get down.'

Otis dismounted, standing a little apart, cautiously flicking his eyes from one man to the other.

47

Derek turned his back on all of them and slowly pulled the gun from his belt. Near what had been the bunkhouse was a partially-burned piece of pine board with a knot near the center of it. He cocked the gun, aimed briefly, and fired. The board was jarred slightly and the knot flew out.

Cervantes said with satisfaction, 'It is good. But it is not the way.' He removed to the remains of the ranch house wall, picked up a charred ember and with deft precision sketched the outline of a man on the planks. He turned, stepped off ten paces and spun about, the gun blasting almost before he'd made the full turn. Three leaden balls smashed into the silhouette. It would have taken an eight-inch circle to cover the three holes, yet all would have represented solid blows to the chest. 'You see, señor,' he said softly. 'That is the way. To shoot a small mark slowly—that is good when you wish to kill a deer. But a man is different; one assumes that he also has a gun.'

Derek wet his lips. 'One of you mentioned a man's name—Lashner. Is he faster and more accurate than you?'

Cervantes shrugged sadly. 'I do not know him, señor. But from what one hears he is faster and more accurate than anyone.'

'I'll keep that in mind,' Derek said. 'But I think we've talked enough about guns. I'd like to see the ranch now. Then I want to start clearing the debris from the house, and after that we'll rebuild the pens.'

'What about those supplies you were talking about?' Griff demanded.

Derek said softly, 'I'll go to La Partida in about three days for the first wagonload. And after that I'll do all the worrying about supplies. You'll simply do as you're told.'

CHAPTER FIVE

At the sight of Griff and Cervantes entering the store, Hees slapped both hands violently down on the counter. 'You fools! I waited three days wondering what the hell happened. And then two hours ago the Englishman rode in with Otis!'

In his anger he started around the counter toward them, and his elbow nudged a sack of sugar. It fell from the shelf and split its seams. He automatically stooped to pick it up and Griff snickered.

'This is a hell of a business you're in.'

Hees straightened, glowering. 'Let me tell you somethin'. Many's the time I've had dirt like you walk right in here and beg! And I've saw men grub in the dirt year after year and not make enough to buy shoes and a decent set of harness. And I've saw the cow-chasers make do with rawhide and wooden pegs, and eat beef without salt until they was like animals. An' the first nickel they got, they had to bring it to me!'

'Then why the hell do you want to go into the cow business?'

'Because there's money in it now. Delphine Judson proved that. But that don't have a damn thing to do with you and the greaser here. You tell me what happened, an' it better be good!'

Cervantes shot him a burning look. 'Señor, you're excited, no?'

Hees's wide mouth turned down at the corners. 'I'm waitin'.'

Griff set his feet and his voice was stone hard. 'This Englishman's got money over in the bank. We could've shot him and the money would've rotted there—or old Willetts would've got it. But then we got this idea; we can hire a crew with his money. We can use his money to buy supplies with—then when we get ready to make a drive we'll get rid of him. That means up to that point you haven't furnished a red cent.'

Cervantes moved up beside him, his silky voice edged and sharp. 'But for this, señor, we will want more money. We will have saved you much.'

Hees almost exploded. He furiously wiped his hands on his apron. 'You ain't got enough brains between you to wad a shotgun with. One more slip up and you won't get any

50

money. Cain't you see what'll happen? Let him hire a crew and then give him any trouble, and he'll run you out of the country. None of us'll make anything.'

'Hell,' Griff argued, 'we said we'd run the outfit for him; maybe we'll have somethin' to say about the crew he hires.'

'And have you got somebody in mind?' Hees inquired sarcastically. 'The way I heard it, Langston's over to the hotel packin' his things, an' Otis is out hiring a crew amongst his friends.'

'Before you get so damned smart,' Griff wheezed, 'you better think this whole thing out. We don't need you now. The only reason we're willin' to keep you in with us is because everybody around here owes you money, and you can keep most of 'em from hirin' out to him. That's all you've got to offer now.'

'All?' Hees asked harshly. He rounded the counter and stood so close to them that they were forced to turn and face him. 'You, Cervantes, you're a Mex and I don't like one kind of furriner better'n another kind. You can get run out if there's any need for it. An when you cross the river I'll see to it that the *Rurales* know you're comin'.

'And you, Griff, I don't like you better'n any other Yankee. But we got Yankee troops in Texas now—and I'll use 'em if I have to. And don't think they ain't still lookin' for bounty-jumpers.' He read the hard threat in

51

Griff's eyes and grinned. 'All you got to worry about is a few years in the pen—whatever it's worth for four enlistments in the Yankee army, at twelve hundred dollars a kick. But think what they'll do to Cervantes! He burned a house with a woman in it. And just in case somethin' happens to me, my nephew in Santone knows all about both of you.'

He changed his tone abruptly. The deadliness was still there, but his voice took on an almost pleasant quality as he went back around the counter. 'Never mind, boys, I was just mad is all. We'll get along fine. And we don't have to worry none about Langston, neither.'

He slid a wooden barrel half-filled with trash over beside the split sugar sack, fished a scrap of cardboard from the barrel, and knelt to clean up the mess. He added conversationally, 'When he come in alone, I figgered he'd got rid of both of you, and I'd have to start over again. But I fixed his clock anyways. Some of Delphine Judson's boys was in here a while ago, and I told 'em he was startin' for the ranch this morning. And if I know Delphine, he'll never get there. Her bein' like she is is why I'm willin' to let her have the Strip—as long as I get the rest of it.'

CHAPTER SIX

Delphine Judson was halfway across the ranch yard and approaching the screened door that led to the living room when she heard Billy Cedar say firmly, 'Delphine!'

She stopped and watched him come up to her, a middle-aged man, lean and gray, his face lined and tired and still ornamented with last night's growth of gray beard, even though he'd been up for hours.

Ordinarily Billy Cedar was a man of patience, and politeness was second nature to him. Since they hadn't seen each other all morning she expected him to ask how she felt, and then pass the time of day while he built up to what he wanted to say. Instead he poked his hat back with gnarled hands and said, 'You know what I come to talk to you about.'

The sleeve of her blue jacket made a swishing sound as her elbow slid past her body. She placed her clenched fist into a pocket of her Levis. 'I know, but I don't want to talk about it.' She was aware that the register of her voice had lowered, and she was half-angry at Cedar's unspoken thoughts. Lowering her voice was habit, nothing more; when she'd started doing it, before the war, she might have been trying to overcome the

53

fact that she was a woman only five feet four in her high-heeled boots, and forced always to talk up to every hand on the ranch. But that was no longer important.

The trouble was that Billy Cedar liked to remember her as she had been before the war. He seemed to close his eyes sometimes and refuse to see the Delphine Judson who'd driven a herd of longhorns all the way to Missouri when half the men in the country had failed.

Cedar's eyes squinted. 'You're goin' after that Englishman,' he accused, 'and you've got no more right to do it—and no more call neither—than you'd have to go into La Partida and run out some family you don't even know.'

She said grimly, 'I won't argue about it. I'll do what I think has to be done, and I'll do it thoroughly and that'll be the end of it.'

Cedar's voice neither raised nor lowered. 'You're doin' it to get land that doesn't belong to you. It won't belong to you even if you take it. And there's somethin' else—you must've felt it a time or two already. The crew you've got's all right for a cattle drive, where you don't know what you'll come up against—but not for workin' steady on a ranch. There's too much fight in 'em. One day you'll start somethin' and when you get ready to stop 'em they'll take the bit in their teeth an' keep goin'. They might even do it

54

today.'

She said sharply, 'I've stopped others who were just as bad, and maybe a lot worse, when I had to. And I didn't have any help from you, either! Or anybody else!' She saw him wince and knew she had him silenced. 'You be saddled and ready to go with the rest of us in twenty minutes.'

She turned away from him and went on into the house, letting the door slam behind her. 'Adelita!' she called. 'I'm leaving in a few minutes. I'll have coffee before I go.' She crossed the big living room and entered her bedroom, deliberately trying to shut Cedar's arguments from her mind. She tossed her hat onto the bed and shook out her hair; there, she was calmer already when she could stop to think that the hair needed cutting, that it was getting too long to pile up comfortably under her hat.

She sat down at the dressing table, opened the top drawer for her brush, and stared wide-eyed at the yellow ribbon tucked away in a back corner. Then she remembered that she'd put it there herself when she'd come across it last week. She removed it now, crumpled it, and threw it aside for Adelita to pick up. It was only a silly, sentimental reminder of other days when she'd been a young girl, with two older brothers and a father who had wanted her dressed always in ribbons and flowered dresses, who couldn't stand the thought of her doing any kind of toil, and even wanted to see her ride sidesaddle. But that was before they'd taken her to San Antonio—till the end of the war.

She lifted the brush and raked it across her hair, and at the same time called, 'Adelita! The coffee!'

Her hair was heavy and had a tendency to escape the pins and frame her face in curly tendrils. Today it seemed more unruly than usual, and she brushed savagely at it until she realized that she was only spilling out anger at Billy Cedar.

He was a man with principles, she thought. He could afford to be; he'd never had anything at stake. When her father had taken the bare land and turned it into a ranch, Cedar had been a big help; but he could never have done the same thing for himself, even though he knew more about cattle—and possibly more about handling men—than her father had ever known. He simply lacked the will to own anything, and he couldn't understand it in others.

But that wasn't all, she thought angrily. Things had always been easier for him than for any of the rest of them. He'd stood in battle beside her father and brothers, and hadn't been touched. He'd been off to war, and therefore not here to help when the Comanches had come and burned half the ranch buildings and stolen all her horses. And

56

a year later he could have found Yankee soldiers right here, if he'd been here to look. They'd been after Comanches, they'd said. But they'd driven away her stock and helped themselves to her meager supplies before they'd left.

On both those occasions she had tried to get help from town, but the few men there had been afraid to leave their own wives and families. The third time, when the outlaws with their scraggly beards and dirty clothes had come, she hadn't asked for help.

She felt a tiny shudder crawl up her backbone. They had wanted the same things the others had wanted—and more.

One of them had pulled her from the house and the furious fight she put up all across the yard had only delighted him. His hairy face had scraped across her cheek when he'd lifted her like a sack of meal and flung her over his shoulder. Nobody else was at the ranch house then but Adelita and old Charley Oddman, who had been trying to keep things running these past months, but who now lay, bloody and dying, on the living-room floor.

She felt the man's foul breath on her face as he flung her onto a pile of hay in the barn and began to rip at her clothes. Then her flailing hands found an ax handle and closed over it, and she brought the ax head down against the small of his back with all her strength. Sometimes she could still feel the way he gasped with horror and surprise and pain. And sometimes she could still see him lying there, helplessly moaning, after she struggled out from beneath him and pushed him over to one side. She looked down at him then and knew that death was not always a thing which came easily like a string being snipped. It could be a horrible thing that dragged on and on—but she had known that already. Charley Oddman's death was not coming easy, and the men responsible for it were still in the house. She pulled the outlaw's gun from its holster and started back to the house.

Two of the three other outlaws were in the kitchen forcing Adelita to cook a meal for them. Her first shot blasted a hole in the nearest man's temple, and her second caught the outlaw beside him at the base of the neck. The third man scrambled out of a window and escaped, but he'd carried a leaden ball with him; she knew that later from the splotch of blood on the window sill.

She and Adelita dug two graves that evening. Charley Oddman was buried in one of them, with a neat cross above him; the other three bodies had been dumped into a common hole. That hole was somewhere in the middle of what today was her largest corral. Since then she'd never worn another ribbon. And since then she'd fought tooth and nail, hiring hands on promises, failing on two cattle drives because she was not strong enough but succeeding on the third because she had traveled with what was virtually an army. An army of men who'd been in battle and knew how to fight and liked it.

Well, her ranch had grown stronger and bigger; bigger than it had been even in her father's time. It might grow still bigger in the future, but it wasn't going to grow smaller—not ever. And to hell with Billy Cedar!

Adelita came shuffling through the door, the cup rattling as she set it down on the dresser, disapproval radiating as strongly from her as it had from Cedar. Delphine looked at her broad face framed in the two bright black braids, at her sulky, turned-down mouth and angry brown eyes, and couldn't understand it. Adelita had been here when it had all happened; she had helped dig the graves, had helped bury the men; had cleaned Charley Oddman's blood from the living-room floor. And she had as much cause as Delphine to know that the meek would never inherit the earth as long as a strong man were left alive. She had had a son, Justino, who'd been meek and mild and cheerful. And he had gone off to war with the Judsons and had survived them only long enough to fall at Antietam.

But Adelita said nothing and Delphine was grateful; she didn't feel like another argument this morning. She blew on her coffee, and when the scorching liquid refused to cool quickly enough, she poured it into her saucer and blew over it again. She'd have to hurry now. This morning the Englishman was driving back toward the Tower Ranch alone, with a wagon load of supplies. And she didn't want to miss him. It was better to get it over with quickly. She finished the coffee and stood up, reaching for her hat. 'I'll be back in plenty of time for dinner,' she said.

★   ★   ★

The old grown-over wagon road was beginning to come alive again, Delphine thought. Two horses going to the Tower Ranch and back had already churned up some of the middle ground between the narrow ruts; and now Strick, who'd served as lookout, had motioned that a wagon would come round the bend any moment to freshen up the ruts themselves.

She waved her arm for the men to scatter out across the road to face the oncoming vehicle. With Strick almost up to her now there'd be eight of them behind her when she braced Langston—not the kind of odds a man liked to brag about. But to a woman it didn't matter. At least to her it didn't. One day she'd let a wagon pass—when its reins were held by a man powerful enough to take the rest of the Tower Ranch and hold it and forget about the Strip. But Langston wanted all of it and wouldn't be able to hold any of it.

The wagon moved around the bend, pulled by two horses and followed by a zebra-striped dun. The Englishman tightened the reins, then seemed to realize the hopelessness of his position. He clucked and came on. He was handsome, she thought, and he'd bought clothes in town since she'd seen him fight on the boardwalk that day. He was wearing blue duck pants and a jacket like her own, and sporting a pair of new Texas-type boots to go with his Stetson. He even carried a gun stuck in his belt, and he'd been unarmed before. All these things doubly reassured her that now was the time to get rid of him, once and for all.

He stopped dead in front of her, his blue eyes staring up at her speculatively, his mouth, with its small and trim military mustache, quirked slightly at the corners.

'Get down!' she ordered.

He made no move to comply, but raised his hand to touch the brim of his hat. The gesture made her furious; she couldn't know for sure, but she'd bet a month's pay for her whole crew that tipping a hat was no English custom. He was trying to be like everybody else in this country and that was the very thing that alarmed her most.

Before she could repeat her command Gort, who was gun-happy, sounded off. He was short and dark with heavy black brows and a voice as throaty as a frog's. 'This lady said git down!' he bellowed gleefully, and the rifle at his shoulder exploded. The ball plowed across one of the reins in Langston's hands and it flipped free.

'Gort!' she snapped. 'You'll shoot when I tell you to, not before. You, Pullet—and you, Strick—help the Englishman from his wagon!'

They climbed down and surged forward, six-guns leveled. One clambered up each side of the wagon and grabbed for an arm. Langston made no move for his gun, but he twisted his body and pounded his right fist squarely into Strick's eye. Strick fell back flat on the ground, crying out in rage. But before he could climb back onto the wagon, Pullet had the Englishman on the ground and the two were rolling over and over. The fight lasted only a moment as four other riders left their horses and joined in the melee.

Langston was jerked to his feet and the pistol was snatched from his belt before he was shoved violently forward to stand facing Delphine. Only Billy Cedar and one other hand remained mounted behind her now. Cedar sat with his arms folded in stern disapproval, and Delphine felt some inner satisfaction that he was annoyed.

'Unhitch the horses,' she ordered, 'and turn them loose!'

For the first time Langston spoke. There was bitterness and some derision in his voice. 'Are you doing this so you can keep the Strip—or have you decided to take all of it now?'

'I'll keep the Strip, and keep you off the rest of it.' Beyond him the horses were free now. The wagon tongue plopped into the dirt and she said, 'All right. Now tear up everything!'

'Hell,' Gort argued, 'there's things here we could use. This here's a keg of nails. There ain't no sense in scatterin' 'em all over.'

'We'll take nothing,' Delphine ordered.

'Well, then,' Gort said resignedly, 'we might's well have some fun. Pullet, throw that there kettle up.'

The kettle sailed up into the air and Gort shot a hole in it. A skillet followed, and other assorted utensils, until Gort was forced to stop to reload. Langston piled into him then, and the two of them went down. Gort tried to use his gun as a club, but it was torn from his grasp and flung to one side. Then Pullet joined in and both the Englishman's arms were pinned.

By then the others were yelling and whooping all over the wagon. Flour sacks and sugar and salt containers were slit open. Gort shook the chalk-white flour up in the air and let it settle solidly over them all. In answer he was plummeted with dried peaches and

63

someone swatted him with a bedroll before beginning to slash the quilted cotton into ribbons. Tinned goods were sailed down the road to become rifle and pistol targets. The handles of the shovel and ax were broken, the heads thrown into the brush. The morral and a long length of rawhide *reata* were sliced into bits. Curry combs, brushes and toilet articles were smashed and scattered, whetstones broken, tinware bent and crumpled.

Then all that remained were the frantic dun, a saddle, the revolver, a fine English double shotgun and the wagon itself.

'Gort,' Delphine ordered, 'find the tallest tree around here and put the saddle in the top of it. You, Strick, cut the dun loose and smash the guns.'

'You just hold it!' Billy Cedar bridled. 'There ain't no use in smashin' fine guns like that. Even the Yankees give us our guns and horses to ride home with.'

The dun was already loose and bolting away. 'Smash the guns,' Delphine said.

Langston was on his feet now and he twisted loose, flailing wildly at Pullet. She could almost share his feelings of outrage. The guns were not something he had bought in this country; they were remnants of years past—the last things, perhaps, that tied him to England. She opened her mouth to halt this one act of destruction which was worse than all the others, then held her tongue. The warning Cedar had given this morning was not to be forgotten. The men might refuse to listen and if they did she'd never quite have the upper hand again. She'd have to let it go now, and see that she was never placed in this position again.

Three men downed Langston and sat on top of him as another emptied the revolver in the air, then placed it on a small boulder and smashed at it with a head-sized rock. Gort used the muzzle of the shotgun to dig a small hole beneath the boulder, then pried under the rock until both barrels bent.

The three hands turned Langston loose and he scrambled up, glaring with fury at Delphine. The stare left her ill at ease. By now he should have stood dejected and beaten with no thought but to return to England and forget the whole nightmare of his coming here.

But he might feel that way yet after he'd had time to think about it. She said to Gort, 'You should have saved the ax to smash the wagon with! Roll it over, all of you, and break the axle.'

They heaved on the wagon. It snapped over on its side, hung there for a moment, then flopped onto its back. Repeated smashings with heavy rocks broke out the spokes and finally smashed the axle.

'That's everything,' Delphine said. 'Get on your horses.'

'We could burn it,' Gort protested.

'And the range with it?' Delphine asked coldly. 'Get on your horse!'

They mounted reluctantly, sorry that the fun was over. Delphine waited until all of them were settled before she stared down at the Englishman. 'This is only a warning,' she said. 'If you stay here and hire a crew, I'll fight you with my crew—and there's no better fighters in this country. If you build up your ranch again, I'll burn it like the Comanches did. I'll fight you with every trick I know, and if you don't run, I'll shoot you down. And if you ever try to fight back the whole countryside'll be stirred up against you because you're fighting a woman!'

Derek Langston's blazing eyes searched her face. 'I doubt if anyone in this country thinks of you as being a woman,' he said.

The remark cut, but she laughed and whirled her horse. It was a feeble enough attempt to save face. Nothing he could ever say or do in the future would overcome his walking back into town where he'd ridden out in a wagon with a led horse behind him.

The others moved aside, then fell in behind her as she rode away.

CHAPTER SEVEN

Derek rode into La Partida bareback with the saddle flung over his shoulder. The dun had been easy enough to catch and the saddle not too hard to fish out of a mesquite, but some fool had sliced off his cinch and flung it into the brush. He pulled up in front of the boot shop and slid off the horse.

As he entered the shop, Woodruff's eyes were curious, but the little bootmaker said nothing. Derek held the saddle up beside the counter, aware that he must present a sorry sight if Woodruff could hardly tear his eyes away from him long enough to see what he'd brought in.

The anger was still in him, alternately turning hot and cold. 'Are you a tailor?' he demanded.

Woodruff pushed his chair back in surprise. 'Why, no.'

'Then I'll get somebody else to mend my clothes. You look at the saddle.'

Woodruff stood up and ran his hands over the hard leather. 'Nothin's busted but the cinch,' he said finally. 'It'll be as good as new in about thirty minutes. Maybe less.' He took it and dragged it across the counter and Derek spun on his heel.

He went out vaguely sorry that he'd been

rude but not concerned enough to dwell on it. He was surprised that no one followed him as he moved along the boardwalk. He should be more of a curiosity now than before, he thought, then figured he had the answer. If anyone scrambled after him now they might be dragged into trouble with him.

He turned and entered the general store and surprised a look on Hees's face he couldn't quite fathom. Then Hees grinned, showing bared teeth. His eyes swept with hard amusement over Derek's torn clothing and dirt-smudged face. He had been stacking tinned goods on a shelf, but now he strutted over and stood by the pot-bellied stove, his face alight with satisfaction. 'Guess that about winds you up, don't it?' he asked. 'Or do you figger to be hardheaded and stay till you get killed?'

Derek was suddenly too tired even to nurse the anger any longer. 'I'll need a wagon, horses and supplies,' he said.

'Where's the wagon and horses you had?'

'The wagon's destroyed. I'll have the horses back here within a week.'

Hees's solid face turned cold. 'You can have 'em back here in five minutes or six months. I don't care. I don't care if they ain't never back. You're goin' to pay for 'em and for the wagon, too, 'fore you get any more supplies. I'll take two hunnerd dollars for the wagon and a hunnerd apiece for the horses.'

Derek straightened up in spite of his weariness. He rubbed his palm over the hard knuckles of his left hand. 'The wagon might have been worth forty dollars once, but not recently. The horses—maybe ten dollars each. But that's giving them the benefit of the doubt. You know that.'

Hees said stubbornly, 'I told you my prices. An' you'll pay or you'll get no more supplies—'less you want to travel sixty miles for 'em.'

Derek looked at him speculatively, and at the same time became aware of two townsmen grinning in the doorway. Hees raised his voice for the onlookers' benefit. 'You might's well wake up. You're beat. If I was you I'd see old Willetts, an' then strike out with what money I had left.'

'I'm not leaving!' Derek went over to the counter and looked at the display of guns hanging on the wall. 'I'm beginning to feel the need for a gun, the same as everybody else,' he said. 'I'll buy that Dance revolver and then we'll talk about the rest of it.'

'You ain't buyin' nothin' till you pay for that wagon and them horses,' Hees countered.

Derek turned to face him. 'I'll give you sixty dollars for the lot, and that's more than they're worth.'

'I told you my price!'

Derek looked at the two ragged loafers and

saw that they were ready to back Hees's play if it came to that. The storekeeper had the whole town in the palm of his hand. 'Then I'll pay you nothing, and I'll go somewhere else for my supplies,' he said.

As he went out past the bewhiskered men he heard them sniggering and thought, *They're not even making fun of me. They're only trying to win Hees's approval.*

Willetts was seated complacently behind his desk. Derek went by him, then was angry at himself because he hadn't asked for directions to Otis' house. But now he wouldn't turn back.

Several boys were playing mumblety-peg in a weedy space between two of the buildings. He stopped and watched the knife flip through the air and stick. When they all looked up curiously at him he asked, 'Who can direct me to the Otises?'

One of them, who somehow looked wrinkled and worried and old, though he couldn't have been more than nine, asked suspiciously, 'What you wan 'em fer?'

'Mr. Otis works for me. I have business with him.'

'He ain't in town.'

'Then I'll leave a message with Mrs. Otis.' He smiled down at the worried little face. 'Are you Robert Otis?'

The youngster stood up and hitched his pants. 'Yep.'

Even the boy, Derek thought bitterly, looked at his bare hip for reassurance before he made a move. 'I'll take you right up to the steps,' Robert said. 'Fer a nickel.'

Derek felt in his pocket for the coin and handed it to him solemnly. 'It's a bargain.'

Robert clutched the nickel, the mumblety-peg forgotten. He broke into a rapid trot. 'Come on, mister,' he flung over his shoulder. Derek had to swing at once into a long, steady stride to keep up with him.

At the end of the little town they cut left off the street onto a weedy, littered lot, and angled toward a gray lumber house standing yardless and alone, a homely blotch on the ugly landscape.

But there was no litter about the house itself. The steps and porch looked as scrubbed as they looked weatherbeaten, and even the dog who came up to sniff suspiciously at Derek's boots appeared to have been washed within the last hour.

Mrs. Otis answered his knock by opening the front door only a crack until she saw Robert standing with him.

'This here's Pa's boss,' Robert said.

Derek took off his hat as the door swung wider. Mrs. Otis looked far older than her husband, he thought, and her looks weren't helped by a skin that was deeply creased and sunburnt. But her face was still slim and well-contoured and once she must have been

71

pretty before her baby-soft blond hair had faded to a harsh sandy color, splotched with gray wisps that fell limply from the knot at her neck.

She stepped out onto the porch. Her dress was patched and badly faded, but like everything else here, it was painfully clean. And her eyes, a deep cobalt blue, were bright and alive and as direct as any man's, even now when her bony hands plucked nervously at her apron.

'I'm Derek Langston, Mrs. Otis.' He smiled and held out his hand. 'Robert said your husband's gone out of town.'

Her grip was surprisingly strong. 'That's right.' She hesitated. 'He's out hirin' a man. A real good man. Lives about thirty miles east of here.'

Derek asked slowly, 'Why did he go so far?'

She breathed a sigh and dropped her eyes. 'I dunno if I ought to speak, Mr. Langston,' she said in a tone so low he had to strain to hear it, 'but Sam couldn't git nobody here in town to work fer you.' She looked back up at him and he could see a tinge of fear in the depths of her eyes. 'But I ain't afraid o' Casper Hees and neither is Sam. And Sam knows two-three men that live down the road an' don't owe Casper nothin'—they'll come if he asks 'em. They was together in the war.'

'Is that the only reason nobody here will

work for me—because Hees won't let them?'

She nodded her head violently. 'Before the war,' she said finally, 'we all got along good here. There was two, three big ranches that needed hands, and what with chickens and vegetables, we could trade for what we needed. But most of the good men rid off with Mr. Judson, and little by little Casper raised his prices till it took more 'n' more of what we had just to git the staples. An' then he took to makin' us sign deeds and papers afore he'd give us flour, and what little money our men sent home he wouldn't even take. An' that's why he can make anybody in this town do about anything he says.'

Derek stood uneasily, unable to offer either comfort or promise. He put his hat back on and said, 'When your husband comes back, tell him to take the hands he's hired and go to the ranch. He's to straighten up everything the best he can with what he's got. I'm going to Centro for supplies and I'll be gone about a week.'

Mrs. Otis pushed at her wispy hair. 'You leavin' town?'

'For a week,' Derek repeated.

'Then I'll—I'll give him your message.' She struggled for words. 'I ain't meanin' to be nosy, but—Sam said you was takin' supplies out to the ranch afore he left—an'—an' you look like you had some trouble. I could sew up your clothes a little if you'd let me.'

It was almost the first humane thing anybody had said to him since he'd come to La Partida and Derek felt a choking in his throat. But he shook his head. 'Thanks anyway, Mrs. Otis. I'm in a bit of a rush. Tell Sam I'll see him next week.' He turned and went down the steps, and laid his hand briefly on Robert's head. ''Bye, sonny.' He said over his shoulder, 'Don't you worry, Mrs. Otis,' and started back across the lot.

As Sara Otis watched his long-legged stride take him rapidly toward the street, she was torn between stark worry and the irrational feeling that the tall stranger could take care of himself and the Otises too, in spite of the way he'd been handled by somebody this morning.

'You think he was jumped by Injuns?' Robert asked.

'No, I don't,' she snapped, 'an' don't you go 'round tellin' people 'bout this neither!' And then, because she really was worried, she continued irritably, 'Did you gather up them eggs like I told you? Them hens is laying out away from the house some place and I know there's more eggs'n you found yesterday.'

Robert grimaced. 'Aw, Mom—I was playin' with the other kids!'

'You do like you're told! An' I'll tell you somethin' else—the coyotes got a hen last night, and they caught her roostin' over by them huisache trees. You said you counted

74

'em and they was all here.'

Robert stood abashed and repentant. 'I musta missed one,' he said feebly. He dug into his pocket. 'But look, Ma, I charged that feller a nickel for bringin' him over here and you can have it.'

Her face grew softer. 'No, you keep it and buy yourself some candy. But mind you, don't eat it all at once! Now you go look for them eggs. I'm goin' over to the store.'

'Aw, gee, cain't I do it later? I want to go to the store, too. I mean, now that we got money and ever'thing.'

'All right,' she said gently. 'You can go, too. We'll leave as soon as I see what we can get by with buyin'.'

When she came out of the house again she was still wearing the same worn dress and shoes, but her hair was neater and she had a dark blue shawl draped over her shoulders.

Robert skipped along by her side, the nickel clenched tightly in his fist. 'Gee, Mom, ain't it a good feelin' to have money?'

She nodded. 'Just like before the war.'

He laughed up at her. 'That musta been forever ago—afore I was born even.'

'It was a long time ago,' she admitted with a sigh.

She was glad Hees was alone in the store because he always said unkind things she didn't like for others to overhear.

He grinned at her across the counter.

'Well, if it ain't the rich Mrs. Otis! Come down to buy a few things for some big party you're givin'?'

'I'll just need some dried peaches,' she said, 'and some salt and a pound of flour.'

Hees clucked. 'A pound now, is it? You must be havin' a lot of people at that there party. You, Robert, what's that you got in your hand? A nickel? Figger to buy out my whole stock of candy, I reckon?'

Robert looked at the open jar of striped candy, but it was plain to see that the pleasure had gone out of his purchase now.

The clop-clop of a horse's hoofs was coming up the road and Hees moved closer to the door. As the rider passed, the storekeeper turned around and stared triumphantly at Mrs. Otis. 'There goes your Englishman,' he said. 'That's the last you'll ever see of him.'

Her mouth clamped stubbornly. 'He'll be back. He said he'd be back.'

Hees snorted. 'You're just wishin' and hopin'.'

Mrs. Otis lifted her chin. 'He's got money in Willetts' bank. He didn't draw it out, did he?'

'He can get the freighter to do that next time he comes through,' Hees chuckled. 'An' you know somethin', Mrs. Otis? I ain't sure you kin afford them dried peaches. You and I ain't goin' to do no more egg-tradin' for groceries. When that little dab of money you got runs out you still got to pay cash or you ain't gettin' nothin'. You might's well start packin' your things for a move right now. Tell Otis what I said, will you?'

CHAPTER EIGHT

One week and one day later, timed to coincide with the usual Saturday activity in La Partida, Derek rolled back into town at the reins of the first of three mule-drawn wagons. The wagons were flanked by two nondescriptly dressed riders who carried short-barreled shotguns across their saddles, and one tall rider dressed from head to toe in brown broadcloth and mounted on a magnificent brown stallion. The third man wore a slick-handled six-gun low on his right hip, and his long, narrow, tanned face was pierced by a pair of burning brown eyes that took in every detail on both sides of the street.

He was riding close to the lead wagon which was piled high and followed by Derek's dun. He brought his stallion to a statue-stop when Derek pulled over to allow the other two wagons to pass.

Derek leaned back on the wagon seat. 'We'll stay here a minute or two and listen.'

The other wagons were canvas covered and

77

freshly painted a bright barn red, with green lettering on their sides that spelled out LEON SALTNER AND BROTHER. As they ground to a stop in the center of the street they were quickly surrounded by the crowds of people who were in La Partida to market and visit and generally break up the monotony of their week.

The hubbub of conversation rose to a crescendo of speculation, but the lead driver waited until he was certain that the proper atmosphere of curiosity was aroused before he stood up on his wagon seat and waved his arms.

'Gather around, folks! Ever'body gather around! Come on, folks, gather around! Right here close where you can hear what I've got to say.' The hubbub dimmed, but he continued to wait until all that could be heard was the rattle of harness and the lazy hum of cicadas. Then he threw up both hands like a man about to make a political speech.

'Ladies and gentlemen, what I've got to say won't take long. As you can see on the side of this wagon, I work for Leon Saltner and his brother Josh. Now the Saltner brothers heard somethin' t'other day—the kind of thing they don't like to hear. They heard you all were forced to buy your merchandise in one little ol' store right here in La Partida. They heard you all were gettin' cheated, gypped and overcharged—that you couldn't make a halfway decent trade, and your credit wasn't worth two cents unless you signed away ever'thing you had.

'Well, folks, this here's Leon and Josh's answer to your problem. We'll be here oncet a week from now on. We've got merchandise for sale cheaper than you're used to paying and we're not worried about money. If you've got it, mind you, we'll be glad to get it. But if you don't have it we'll take just about anything you've got in trade except longhorn steers.'

The noise began to rise again and he waved his arms until quiet was restored. 'An' if you don't have money, but you're settled down and tryin' to work a place, then the Saltner brothers want you to know they've got faith in you and in the future of Texas. They'll extend you credit and you won't have to sign nothin' but just your name. Then when you get the money, why you just pay up.

'We'll try this for a few months, folks, and if it works out, why we'll just come and build a store right here in La Partida!' He went on trying to talk, but the cheers that refused to stop drowned out his voice and the surging of the crowd scared his mules and almost upset his wagons.

The stallion was getting restive and the dun behind the wagon was also beginning to shy from the crowd. Derek looked up at his companion. 'I've got business with a man

79

here. You can tie your horse and come with me if you like.'

The tall man nodded, guided the horse in a pivot turn and rode down the street. Derek hitched his mules, then moved to the back of the wagon to calm the dun. Just behind the wagon an excited farmer was tugging at a woman's arm. 'Ma, you git home and pen up them pullets quick!' Then, as she started off, 'No. No. I'll do it. You be pickin' out some clothes for the young'uns!' And he took off at a quick trot.

A moment later the tall, brown-clad man came back. They moved together through the good-natured, laughing crowd until Derek spotted Hees. The storekeeper was furiously stretching his apron with both hands, and his face was swollen with anger.

Derek veered toward him and touched his shoulder. 'Hees,' he said sharply, 'come over to the store. I want to talk to you.' He didn't wait to see if he were followed but turned at once and went into the empty store.

Hees hadn't hesitated; his heavy footsteps hit the boardwalk before Derek and his companion were more than just inside the doorway. 'You—you're responsible for this!' Hees raged. His eyes raked Derek from head to foot, took in the smooth .44 Remington he now wore in a slick holster at his hip, then moved over to the long arms and big hands of his companion.

'I'll introduce you,' Derek said. 'Casper Hees. Rig Lashner. Lashner works for me now.'

Hees's eyes widened, then quickly narrowed. The fury was still there, but fear was mixed in with it now as he backed toward the counter, his mouth tightly clamped and his hands in plain sight.

'I've come to pay you for that wagon,' Derek continued. 'The one I bought in Centro is better than the one you rented me. It cost me forty dollars. I'll give you thirty-two for yours and take a receipt.'

For a long minute Hees seemed unable to move. Then he walked heavily around the counter, got a pencil and paper, and scribbled a receipt. He handed it to Derek, who slowly counted out the money. The procedure seemingly restored Hees's bad temper. 'This was a good place to live till you come here,' he said darkly. 'It'll be a good place again after you're gone.'

Lashner moved forward threateningly, but Derek waved him back. 'He's only talking for his own benefit,' he said. He pocketed the receipt and started out.

Lashner held back. His left thumb slid inside his belt and his fingers spread fanwise as he looked at Hees.

From the doorway Derek said, 'Our business here is finished.'

The thumb under Lashner's belt massaged

81

a spot on his stomach for a brief moment; then he dropped his hand to his side and reluctantly started for the door.

Outside the crowd was still fingering through the merchandise at the wagons and Derek was so absorbed in the spectacle that for a moment he almost failed to see Otis coming up the boardwalk, followed by two strapping men as big as he.

'I sure am glad to see you,' Otis said fervently. 'Ol' Hees just about had Sary convinced you wasn't comin' back.' His long face lost some of the worried creases and he gestured at his two companions. This here's Ben Ridge and Jack Jackson—the two fellers I hired to work for you.'

Derek shook hands with each in turn. 'Glad to know you,' he said. He inclined his head. 'This is Rig Lashner.'

To Lashner's evident enjoyment all three men recoiled. He made no move to shake hands, but nodded shortly.

'Didn't you get my message?' Derek asked. 'Why aren't you at the ranch?'

'That's just the whole thing,' Otis protested. 'I reckon Griff and Cervantes figgered you wasn't comin' back neither. They run us off the minute we showed up. They got another feller with 'em an' they say there'll be more droppin' in off and on for the next month or so. They said if you was fool enough to come back out there, you'd get buried there.'

Ridge and Jackson nodded, backing Otis' statement. Studying them Derek saw that they, like Otis, weren't fighters. But that would be no problem for a while. 'Saddle up your horses,' he said. 'We'll go to the ranch right now.'

Otis stood still, hulking and uncomfortable. 'You remember what I said about fightin',' he reminded.

'I remember. You can stop short of the ranch and wait till it's over if you like.'

Otis turned grimly away. 'Come on, fellers. We'll meet right here in five minutes.'

Derek let Otis drive the wagon and rode out of town on the dun because for two days he'd been waiting for the right time to speak to Lashner, and there'd never be a better time than this minute. He motioned at the gunman and they moved forward well in advance of the wagon, leaving Ridge and Jackson to act as outriders.

It was midmorning and a cold breeze was blowing across the flatlands. There was more than a hint of showers in the air and in the sky ahead of them white clouds chased each other across the sun. Derek pulled up the collar of his brush jacket and buttoned it high on his neck.

'Lashner,' he said abruptly, 'I haven't told you yet why I hired you.'

Lashner's usually inscrutable face showed

surprise. 'What do you mean?' he asked suspiciously.

'You think I hired you because you're a gunman—and I did. But not because I want you to kill anybody.'

Lashner half-turned in the saddle, the deadpan expression back in place. 'What the hell are you talkin' about?'

'Just this. I've been told you can draw and fire a gun faster than any other man in this country. I want you to teach me how to do the same.'

Lashner's voice was hollow. 'You mean—you mean that's all you hired me for?'

'That's it.'

'Well, I'll be damned!' For a full minute the gunman seemed to study the idea, then he said slowly, 'Learnin' a quick-draw ain't like nothin' you ever did before. A man's got to practice day in and day out till his muscles get like boils and then get tougher'n rawhide. It looks like a little thing, but just when you get to thinkin' you're good you learn somethin' else. A little short cut maybe, and ten of them short cuts wouldn't add up to a little piece of a second.' He shook his head. 'I don't know's how you'd ever practice hard enough to get real good.'

'I'd practice harder than anybody ever did,' Derek said. 'And I'm just as serious about it as you ever were. And I'll make you a promise—if the day ever comes when I can match you, I'll give you a hundred dollar bonus.'

Lashner drew back as if he'd been slapped. The idea of somebody being that fast was something he didn't even want in another man's mind. But after a moment he saw the humor of it. 'What makes you think I won't let you beat me just to collect the hundred dollars?' he demanded.

'Because the day we have a contest, it'll be in front of people. And your pride won't let you lose just for the sake of the money.'

Lashner's mouth drew flat. 'Then I'll make you a promise, mister. I'll work with you harder'n I ever worked with anybody in my life. I'll try ever'thing I know to make you faster'n me. And if you ever get to the point where I think you might be, I'll make you prove it. You can bet your life on that.'

★   ★   ★

A thin wisp of smoke filed upward from the ranch-house chimney as Derek and Lashner rode into the clearing. The clop-clop of their horses must have been evident for the last several hundred yards and Derek was not surprised to see Cervantes framed in the doorway.

The Mexican made a signal and stepped outside, followed by Griff and another man. None of them carried rifles this time;

probably they thought he'd be easy enough to handle with six-guns. The three spread out fanwise as Derek and Lashner pulled up their horses and swung down.

Griff stood in the middle and Derek stopped directly in front of him, Lashner at his side. 'You ran my men off,' he said, 'and kept them from doing work that needed to be done. You're fired! And you, Cervantes, you're fired, too. And you can take your friend with you when you go.'

Griff said hoarsely, 'I tried to be fair with you. I sent you word you'd be buried if you came back.'

Derek shrugged. 'There's room in the ground for all of us.' Each of them tensed, and each spread the fingers of his right hand. 'The last time I was here,' Derek added, 'you mentioned Rig Lashner. This time I brought him with me.'

None of them reacted, but in the second of silence that followed Derek could hear the wagon rumbling to a stop somewhere far behind him.

'Mike,' Griff said finally, 'we're fired. Why should we face Lashner when it'd be easier to catch Langston off by himself?'

'You are right, Joe,' Cervantes said. 'We will get our horses and we will go. Today we have but one friend with us. But tomorrow we will have two. In a month it will be ten. Or perhaps twenty.'

'A month from now,' Derek said, 'I'll have ten men—perhaps twenty. If you ever come on my property again there'll be no talk. Only guns.'

Cervantes' mouth curled. 'It is said that no man can dispute the Señor Lashner. Perhaps that is so. But perhaps, too, there are things he does not understand. One day we will talk with him. But not now, I will get the horses.' He brazenly turned his back on Lashner and moved off toward the rear of the ranch house. The other men stood fast, waiting.

A few minutes later Cervantes came back riding a coal-black stallion and leading two bays. As Griff and his friend mounted, the Mexican said pleasantly, 'Do not forget, Señor Lashner. There are things you do not understand—but one day we will tell you everything.'

He whirled the stallion and galloped off down the road, racing Griff and the other man. It was only after they'd passed Otis and the wagon without stopping that Derek realized how tense he had been.

But Lashner had seemingly lost interest. His eyes roved over the charcoal figure Cervantes had drawn on the wall and he looked hard at Derek. 'You might as well start learnin' right now,' he said. Simultaneously his gun came out and three booming reports rolled together. The three new holes that appeared inside the charcoal lines, in the area where a man's heart would be, could easily have been covered by the knuckles of a small fist.

Lashner grinned. 'That was to show you that I know what I'm talkin' about.'

Derek started to pull his own gun out, but Lashner said harshly, 'No! You're goin' to do this thing like I say. There's good ways to learn and bad ways, and I don't want you developin' any bad habits. Now—the first thing you'll learn is the swing of it. An' the way you're goin' to practice, that'll only take a week. And you keep this in mind—durin' this week, you ain't in no hurry.'

Derek let his gun slide back into its holster. 'Show me then,' he said.

Lashner grinned sourly, exposing his long teeth. 'First I'll tell you some things. You've got to know where your gun is or you'll never git it out in a hurry. You've got to be so sure your hand'll find it that you won't even think about it. And you've got to be so sure it'll pop out just right that you won't think about that neither. And while the hammer's fallin' you've got to know where the bullet's headed. Now spread your fingers and put your hand out where you can slap at that gun butt.'

Strangely enough the man was a good teacher. After the first few tries Derek began to gain confidence; but before he'd drawn a dozen times he began to realize that there were more fine points to gun fighting than he'd ever imagined. It was strange—he'd

But by comparison with Lashner, he'd moved like a man in a dream.

The wagon was pulling up behind him now. Otis set the brake and climbed down slapping at his clothes. 'I heard shootin',' he said, 'but it was after Griff and Cervantes lit out.' It was more of a question than a statement. Then he saw the three new bullet holes and his eyes widened. 'I guess I see now,' he said quietly.

Lashner refused even to favor him with a glance. Instead he glared at Derek. 'You goin' to stop now, mister?' he demanded.

'Just for a minute. Otis, you can start unloading. I'll be with you in about an hour.'

Ridge and Jackson, who had remained behind the wagon, instantly pitched in, but Otis stood looking curiously at Derek. 'What're you two doin'?' he asked.

'Lashner's teaching me how to fast-draw. In the future I'll be practicing an hour in the morning and another hour in the afternoon. During the rest of each day, I'll want you to teach me what I need to know about the cattle—roping, branding, holding a roundup, and all the rest of it.'

Otis laughed. 'Sounds like you're diggin' in solid. How soon do you figger on makin' a drive?'

'In April. That'll be the important one. But we'll make others later in the summer. By then there'll be a railroad in Kansas.'

Otis lowered his brows. 'Where'd you hear about that?'

'In London.'

Otis cocked his head in disbelief. 'How come they know over there what's goin' to happen in Kansas, when there ain't even nobody around here knows it?'

'Because nobody around here put up the money for it,' Derek answered.

Lashner said savagely, 'I've been waitin' around long enough. Let's get on with it!'

★　　　★　　　★

Lashner's prediction had been almost right. For the first five days Derek Langston's muscles had protested his every move. But the soreness was leaving now and he had a lot to show for a week that had swept by with the speed of a dust devil. The charred upper boards of the ranch house had been cleared away, and the area around the house freshly raked. A corral of crooked mesquite logs had been completed this morning, ready to hold the first of hundreds of cattle which had never

been branded. And the cattl   the
skinny, rolling-eyed longl
ceased to look ugly to him. 7
rope had settled squarely ove
one for the first time and he'd u
critter looked downright pretty.

Sam Otis had laughed. 'You caught a gust
of wind just right!' But he'd added, 'For a
greenhorn, you're doin' pretty good at that!'

But it was Lashner's grudging praise that
really stirred him. They were standing beside
a cleft in a low foothill a half mile from the
ranch when Derek made the practice draw
that caused the gunman to glower at him.

'All right,' Lashner said. 'You've got the
swing of it. An' I ain't seen many men that
had it better. Now you get over and practice
on that stump. And this time you do it fast.
An' I don't mean pretty fast—or as fast as you
can do it and keep comfortable. I mean
you've got muscles and you can use 'em, and
you hit that gun hard and get it out! And if
you don't hit the stump you've to draw ten
times without shootin'!'

They walked to within a few yards of the
stump and Lashner said, 'Now!'

Derek slapped the gun, whipped it out and
fired.

A chip flew from the stump, but Lashner's
lips curled in a tight grin. 'It ain't so smooth
when you do it fast, is it?' he taunted. 'Now
do it again. Faster and smoother!'

The gun snaked out and fired and again chips flew from the stump.

'Next time do it like this,' Lashner said. The words seemed still be hanging in his mouth when his own gun was out, blasting twice. Both bullets thudded solidly into the stump. Lashner held the gun ready to cock a third time and said, 'If you're smart, you noticed something. You noticed that I don't fool around when I'm out here practicing any more than I would if I was tryin' to kill a man. I don't fool around even oncet. Whenever I pull this gun it comes out fast and it shoots straight. That way when the time comes for me to face somebody I'll know I'm doin' the best I can. Now you try it again. And you're not aimin' at the edge of that stump. You're shootin' for the middle.'

The six-gun had barely slipped back into place when Lashner said, 'Now!'

This time it snaked out faster and smoother and the thud of the ball into the stump was a solid thuck.

Lashner said harshly, 'Don't move sideways when you shoot! Movin' takes time! Keep your feet stock-still, and don't ever change your mind after you start to draw. You'll only fumble!' Then his eyes were filled with speculation and his tone grew softer. 'You're goin' to be ready sooner'n I thought,' he said quietly. 'Lots sooner.'

When they rode in a short time later there

92

was a strange horse ground-tied in front of the ranch house. The cowboy sitting in the doorway rose lazily and leaned on the jamb for a time as they approached, then slowly walked over to meet them.

'One of you Langston?' he asked.

Derek nodded as Lashner continued on toward the corral.

'Name's Forrest. I'm just driftin' through.'

Derek swung down and shook his hand. 'Looking for a job?'

Forrest looked briefly after Lashner, then shook his head. 'Not for a spell.'

'Well, you're welcome to spend the night and rest your horse.'

'Thanks. I reckon I'll do that. And say, I might do you a turn. I stopped over to Sam Corenson's place up north of here a week or so ago, an' he said tell anybody I met that he was startin' a drive to Missouri about the middle of March. He's tryin' to make up a big outfit an' he'd be glad to have you with him.'

Derek carefully searched the man's face. 'They're saying around here that if I want to play it safe, the middle of April is too early.'

'Maybe so,' Forrest said. 'But Corenson played it safe last year and still didn't make it. Now he's backed up against a wall.'

'So am I,' Derek admitted. 'But it's not quite the same wall. I have a little more time.' He nodded toward the doorway. 'Go in and pour yourself some coffee. I'll put up my

93

horse and be with you in a few minutes.'

But he spoke again before Forrest had fully turned. 'What will Corenson do if he fails again?'

'Why, he won't be able to hire hands on promises next time—not with more and more people payin' hard cash. So he'll come back and squeeze in a few steers with somebody else's herd, and try to get a stake so he can strike out big again.'

Derek nodded slowly. 'It's what I'd do, too, if things were different. As it is, I'll have only one chance, so I'll have to do it right. But it's not the drive I'm worried about—at least not the biggest part of it. Someone once told me that if I could stick it out, round up a herd, and drive it forty miles, I'd make it all the way to Kansas. I'm beginning to see what he meant.'

Forrest started to answer, but his attention shifted toward an oncoming rider, and Derek followed his gaze. It was Otis.

The cowboy spurred into a gallop when he saw that he was the center of attention. He stopped almost on top of Derek, grinning down at him.

'I don't know but what you might make out around here after all,' he sang out. 'I just talked to a cowboy named Gort, and he come over here to bring an invite from Delphine Judson. She'd be pleased to have you come for dinner tomorrow night.'

Derek smiled slightly. 'Well, then since Gort didn't wait for an answer, he must have been pretty sure I'd accept, don't you think?'

Otis' forehead wrinkled at once. 'Why, yeah, I reckon he was. You're goin', ain't you?'

Derek swung up onto the dun. 'Yes, I'm going.' He looked down at Forrest. 'With just a little luck, I might make that first forty miles after all,' he said.

CHAPTER NINE

It was four o'clock in the afternoon, two hours before Derek Langston was supposed to arrive, and Delphine Judson had already spent more than an hour preparing herself for the meeting. At first her preparations had been pleasant and easy. After she'd fixed her nails she'd taken a long lazy bath with gleaming perfumed crystals saved from before the war. Then Adelita had brushed her hair until every last strand seemed to fall naturally into place. But now she sat in front of the large dressing table mirror, nude from the waist up, staring at herself in humiliation.

She knew that her face was pretty, that her features were nice. God knew, she'd been told often enough during the trips she and her father and brothers had made to San Antonio before the war. And the reflection showed plainly that her stomach was flat and hard and that her breasts were full and high.

But her face was tanned from the sun and the tan extended down into a sharp V between her breasts because she always wore shirts open at the collar. And her breasts and the rest of her body were milk-white and the only fine dress she had was cut low across the full width of her shoulders. Her hands were tanned, too, much more than her arms. But mitts would hide that. If only she could find some way to erase the V below her neck.

For the hundredth time she dipped her finger tips in a bowl that contained the glycerin and rose water prepared in exact accordance with the instructions in *Godey's Lady's Book*, and then tried to rub away the V. When that failed she added rice powder over the solution, and it made a horrible mess, and she had to wash off all of it with a damp cloth.

She spun around. 'Adelita!'

The big Mexican woman must have been just outside the door. She shuffled solidly into the room, stared and said, 'You are two colors.'

She felt like exploding with fury, but instead she almost cried. 'Damn it! I know I'm two colors. And I can't do anything about it. I want you to fix my dress so it doesn't look so bad.'

'You are going to much trouble for the Senor Langston,' Adelita observed.

'And I'll go to even more trouble if I have to! Get my dress out of the closet and let's see what we can do with it.' She grimaced. She shouldn't have been quite so sharp; not when her fury was really directed at Derek Langston and Billy Cedar. Langston because he'd put her in this impossible situation and Cedar because he'd persuaded her to go through with this meeting. Well, maybe she wasn't being fair. There were many reasons for seeing Langston besides Billy Cedar's desire for peace. The fact that he'd even come back after she and her crew had humiliated him and after Hees had refused to sell to him was enough to show her that he was more of a man than she had thought. And the fact that he had enlisted Saltner to ruin Hees's business showed that he was imaginative as well. But hiring Rig Lashner was something else again.

She had men on her own crew who had killed before and would kill again. But they weren't like Lashner. He was insane and his biggest pleasure in life came from killing. Not one man on her crew would willingly face him alone; and worse, if Langston hired one killer he would hire others. There would soon be ambushes, and then murder would run rampant through the whole country. Maybe Langston wanted it that way—or maybe he

97

thought she did. In either case Billy Cedar was right; they had to have a meeting.

Adelita brought the dress and Delphine held her arms straight up while the Mexican woman slipped it over her head. 'I don't have my petticoats on,' she protested.

'There is time for that. First we will fix the dress.'

But when it was on, and her hair flung back into place, Adelita surveyed her and clucked. The white moire dress, hand-screened with dark red roses on green leaves was high-waisted and tight over her breasts, with a billowing full skirt. But the beauty of the dress only made the contrasting tanned V below her neck look more ridiculous. She was ready to cry.

'You have a white silk scarf,' Adelita said soothingly. 'I will sew it into the front.'

'Then do it!' she said. She struggled out of the dress and began to pat more glycerin and rose water on the tanned area, hoping she wouldn't be too pressed for time. There was still her hair to brush back into place, the green ribbon to be tied just so, the last-minute inspection of the living room, a check to make certain there were no water spots on the wine-glasses, and a last glance to make sure the logs in the fireplace were stacked just right. And a dozen other things she'd think of between now and then. It was five years since she'd had a guest. Once the

Judson ranch had been crowded with friends, but how few had come back after Appomattox!

After the dress was fitted properly it still looked patched and a full hour had been wasted. It took more precious minutes to adjust the petticoats, to pull on the silk stockings and slip into the satin shoes. And then it was time to begin checking everything and it was already six o'clock and she heard the dogs bark as a horse moved steadily across the ranch yard. One of the hands quieted the hounds and went back into the bunkhouse.

It was dark outside now and the lamps in the living room cast a yellow oblong through the window beside the door. She looked out and saw Derek Langston dismount and immediately felt uncomfortable and ill at ease. Somehow, in spite of her own preparations, she'd thought of him as dressed in the brush jacket and jeans he'd worn when she saw him last. Instead he wore tight-fitting gray pants, high boots that were slick and shiny black, and a well-tailored Prince Albert coat that she knew must have been very expensive.

He hesitated for a moment and she took hope. He must also be feeling misgivings now; the gun he wore looked out of place with this costume and he must suddenly have become aware of it. And his spurs. He must have forgotten about them until this minute.

He removed them at once and tucked them in a saddlebag. But he hesitated before taking off the gun and hanging it over his saddlehorn. In spite of the short time he'd been in the ranch country, the gun was already hard to part with. He hitched the horse, gave it a little pat, and strode toward the house. She moved hastily away from the window.

She still felt faint twinges of misgivings as she opened the door, but as the light shone full on his face and she saw his expression change from indifference to admiration, confidence in herself came back. 'I'm glad you could come, Mr. Langston,' she smiled.

He looked down at her gravely. 'I'm glad you invited me.'

She moved aside for him to pass and softly closed the door behind him. He cast an appreciative glance around the big living room with its sturdy overhead beams, at the Spanish tapestries on the walls, at the silver and glass gleaming on the small table near the fire.

'This is the first home I've been in since I came to Texas,' he said. 'It was well worth waiting for.'

'Thank you.' Adelita was already shuffling in from the kitchen and Delphine smiled. 'It must all be quite different from England.'

Adelita carried in the last of the steaming dishes and pointed toward the table with her head. 'Eat,' she said, and turned heavily and clumped from the room.

He smiled and pulled out Delphine's chair. 'Different—yes. But I think I'll like it here—without reservations of any kind.'

'You might—if you stayed long enough.' She hadn't meant it as it sounded, but it was too late to withdraw the words.

He sat across the table and lifted his napkin. When he answered his voice was pleasant enough, but it nevertheless held a fine note of determination. 'I plan on staying. I intend to convince everyone of that.'

She was grateful that it was time to eat, and therefore not necessary to reply. She'd had Adelita fix a Mexican dinner—not only because she did it really well, but also because it all could be put on the table at once, and she was pleased when Derek seemed to enjoy it despite its unfamiliarity.

She purposefully kept the table conversation light, and found herself savoring the small talk, found the years slipping back to gentler times, till she almost felt herself listening for her father and brothers.

When the last of the dessert was gone, she moved over to the decanter and he pushed back his chair and stood beside her. She poured two glasses of brandy and lifted one toward him, uncomfortably aware of a strange tingling sensation as his fingers brushed hers.

She moved back and sank onto the couch

facing the fire, hoping he'd sit beside her. But he took the glass and put it on the mantel, looking up at the sword that hung on the wall, and at the dark daguerreotype just beneath it.

'It was my father's sword,' she said. 'And the picture is of him and my two brothers.' She hesitated. 'They were all killed in the war—all on the same day—at a place called Shiloh.'

'Sam Otis told me that,' he said gently. 'I'm sorry.'

Her voice took on an edge. 'The Texans spent ten years trying to get this state into the Union, and a few years later they did their best to get out. It didn't make much sense to me then, and it doesn't now. But two things I'm sure of. A lot of good men were killed in the war, and the ones who came back aren't the same as they were before.'

He nodded. 'I know.'

She looked up at him curiously. 'Do you, Mr. Langston? Were you ever in a war?'

'Yes. Yes, I was a cavalry officer for years. But I doubt if anyone over here ever heard of most of our battles and skirmishes.'

'Were they so easy and one-sided, then? The British against the natives?'

He smiled ruefully. 'They were one-sided, right enough, but not often in our favor. They were six to one against us at Delhi, and behind some pretty enormous fortifications at that. And at Balaclava, we were only a brigade of Light Cavalry charging heavy guns with a murderous fire pouring into both our flanks.'

She stared in spite of herself. 'You were in the charge of the Light Brigade?'

'Yes. I was one of almost seven hundred who charged down the valley, and one of the lucky two hundred who came out.'

She was quiet for a moment or two, listening to the crackle of the logs. Then she said, 'My foreman, Billy Cedar, was with my father and brothers. He was one of the lucky ones, too. He's still a fighter when he has to be, but he hates war of any kind. Do you feel the same way?'

He lifted his glass from the mantel and held it up. 'I hate unnecessary fighting— unnecessary killing. We'll drink to that, if you like.' He touched the brandy to his lips. 'Spanish,' he said appreciatively after a minute, 'unless the Mexicans have become very adroit at carrying on a heritage from the old country.'

'It's Spanish,' she said. 'Are you so familiar with brandy that you can recognize all of it? Where it comes from? Who made it?'

He laughed. 'It's the fashionable thing in some places.'

She could almost visualize herself in one of those fashionable places, and suddenly she was afraid that the pleasant atmosphere of unreality here would vanish. 'You were telling me about the battle,' she said. 'Please don't stop.'

'But I had stopped.' He looked at her quizzically. 'I assume I was invited here to talk about cattle and land. Or possibly about my intentions to remain here.'

'Please—not yet.' The atmosphere was shattered, but it only made her resolve harder to put off the unpleasantness just a little longer. She hadn't given in to anyone for any reason since the day she'd killed that man in the barn, and now, when she had a compromise to offer, she couldn't bring herself to say so—not yet. 'I'd like to hear about a battle where no one I know got killed,' she said fiercely.

He set the glass back down on the mantel and crossed his hands behind his back. 'I suppose I could tell you some of it, then. We had five hundred casualties that day, but you didn't know any of them.'

She flushed scarlet. 'I'm sorry. I didn't mean it that way. It's just—it's just that so many men I knew got killed. There's almost no place you can mention up and down the Mississippi or in the Shenandoah Valley that isn't the grave of a friend.'

'I'm sorry, too. I shouldn't have said it that way. And it was all a long time ago—I've almost forgotten some of it. But the part that sticks in my mind has to do more with the

104

horses than the men. I've told you that the Russians were firing at both our flanks and blazing away in front of us. But it was enormously important that we hold formation. And we did it—when comrades on both sides of us dropped from their saddles we closed up and went on. The horses, of course, were struck as often as the men. Some were maimed and screaming and frantic. But they tried to maintain formation, too, even when they were shot to pieces.' He was silent for a moment, his eyes looking past her. 'We rode in and silenced the Russian battery and turned and fought our way out. The whole attack took only twenty minutes, and it was all a mistake.'

She stared in disbelief. 'A mistake?'

He shrugged. 'Our commander was on a hill high above us. He could see several batteries, but we could see only one. Somehow his communication to us was misunderstood, and we silenced the only guns we could see. It wasn't what he had in mind.'

She sat unable to speak for an uncomfortable moment, then nervously rose and crossed to the mantel for his glass. She lifted it and turned toward him, keeping the glass between them. The story had left her moved, and a feeling of sympathy welled up in her. But she stared up at him and saw by the hardness in his eyes that he wanted no sympathy. And she realized, too, that it was

105

something she'd never intended to give. Bringing him here had been as cold-blooded as anything she had ever done; he was a man alone in a wild country and she was a pretty woman. For most men that would have been enough.

But she should have known that he was used to women who were more charming, more polished, not so provincial. She was angry with herself because she couldn't attract him and thus serve her purpose, and at the same time she was hurt because he attracted her in spite of everything, and wouldn't respond.

Then some of the harshness went out of his face and his head moved almost imperceptibly down toward her. It was a victory and she moved at once toward the brandy decanter.

But the victory was short lived. When she turned toward him with the refilled glass he seemed to have forgotten it already.

'Maybe you'll tell me something,' he said. 'Maybe you'll tell me why you destroyed my equipment and made a fool of me.'

She held out the brandy and he took it. 'Because I wanted the Strip,' she said simply.

'Why? You have a great deal of land already—as much as you can control.'

She shook her head. 'You're wrong. I can control more—lots more. And at least nine months a year, the Strip has water on it. It's good grazing land, and you can't shake a bush without flushing a longhorn.'

'And it meant nothing that I had title to it?'

She said firmly, 'Nothing. Because I didn't think you could keep any part of the ranch. I thought if I gave you back the Strip, we'd both lose it.'

'Then one might say you were testing my strength.'

'Not really. I—I just took it for granted you were weak.'

He edged closer, towering above her, and she grew confused. 'And what do you think now?' he asked.

'Well, I—I know what you did to Casper Hees. I know that you brought in Rig Lashner; that you've hired other people to work for you—and you were wearing a gun when you rode here tonight. I saw it. But I don't understand why—'

She took a step back from him and moved over to the mantel. She looked up at the sword, and then at the picture of her father and brothers. 'I mean—they fought the Indians, outlaws, everybody—because they loved the land. It was their country and they were a part of it.'

'It's my country, too, now,' he said.

She gripped the mantelpiece with both hands. 'But there are some ways you'll be different.'

'Different?' he asked harshly. 'How different?'

His face was heavily lined with shadows as she turned toward him. 'Well, for one thing, there's this deed you keep talking about. Sometimes here—we just shake hands, is all. And it means more to us than a piece of paper ever could.'

'Is that what you want to do now—shake hands? Because if you're leading up to some sort of offer, then make it and let's quit fencing.'

She walked slowly back toward the couch—everything depended on this moment now. She sank onto the cushions and leaned back, and was glad when he came and stood beside her. 'Yes,' she said. 'Yes. I had an offer in mind. The Strip is yours and I'm willing to let it stay that way.'

He asked impatiently, 'That's all there is to it? You're giving up all claim to my land?'

'No—no, that isn't all. I told you, it's thick with cattle and I—well, I've guarded all of it for two years now. Kept anyone else from moving in. My men have ridden the Strip the same as they have the rest of my land. They've killed mountain lions there—killer lions. And they've pulled cattle from bog holes and done lots of other things.'

'And you want me to pay you for this?'

'No. I want to make one drive. Gather what cattle I can from the Strip in two days—and what's left and the land is yours. And there'll be no more trouble between us.

Nothing like—the other day.' She sank further back on the cushions and her mouth parted. She had not intended to let him touch her but only to take advantage of the fact that he might want to. Now she didn't care. It had been almost five years since a man had kissed her, and almost that long since she'd felt gentleness from anyone except Adelita and Billy Cedar.

But the sternness in him turned to anger and his face grew red. 'Did you think all you had to do was part your lips and I'd forget everything else? There are women in La Partida for that—I don't need you. The land is mine and I'll keep it.'

She felt a heavy thud in her breast as though her heart had skipped a beat. Her skin turned hot all over and she came to her feet and slapped his face. 'Get out! I don't have to make bargains with you!' Her voice rose higher and she couldn't control it. 'I can run you out and Rig Lashner with you! And I'll do it! You'll never get one longhorn off the Tower Ranch! Get out!'

He said roughly, 'You'll no more run me out now than you did before. And you keep off the Strip. It's mine and I'll fight for it. There's only one other thing—since you seem to attach such importance to being a woman, I'd hate for the evening to be a complete loss to you.'

Before she could draw back he had placed

one hand over her head and the other under her chin. She was drawn to him and his lips pressed hard down on hers. After the first moment of shock, she struggled and he released her suddenly, throwing her off balance. If he had said something then, maybe some parting remark to have taken a little of the sting out of his words, she might even have forgiven him. But he seemed to have forgotten her as he turned about, quietly opened the door and disappeared into the darkness. She stood for a long moment unable to move, and then his horse was galloping across the ranch yard.

She sank down onto the couch. This was the kind of moment when women were supposed to cry, but no tears would come to her eyes.

CHAPTER TEN

The bright moon filled the clearings with sifted light, and every shrub cast a long shadow. The trees that passed him by were a ghostly parade, but Derek Langston's mind was not concerned with dangers that might strike from the darkness. He was thinking that a kiss was only a small thing and he would not give it credit for the tensions that filled him now. He'd kissed other women and wanted them, and Delphine was no different from the others.

But she was, really. Different in some ways he couldn't describe and in some ways that he could. Thinking back now, he could remember other women who had been ambitious—women with marriageable daughters, women with husbands who could be pushed toward wealth and position, women ambitious for their educated but lackadaisical sons—and all of them had used subtle indirection to flatter and praise and ingratiate. But Delphine wasn't pushing someone else toward success; and her attempt tonight with the art of indirection had been about as subtle and indirect as a longhorn steer stampeding through the brush. She was a woman who seemed proper in a brush jacket, but not in a hand-screened white moire gown, with firelight flickering off silver and glass in the background. She was too hard for that.

But he knew one thing now. He wouldn't give up the Strip—not for a two-day drive or one that lasted an hour. She'd said her father and brothers had fought for the land, so she ought to understand. It wasn't the dirt beneath his horse's hoofs nor yet a green lush stretch of it called the Strip that mattered, but all the things that went with it, the things that made up a way of life.

His fingers slapped the butt of the gun at

111

his waist and it snaked out with a free and easy rhythm. He hadn't believed it at first, but the gun was a part of this life, and he'd have to give Lashner credit—the man was a good teacher. He didn't like his job; he preferred being bodyguard and executioner. But there was no need for that, no need to bring fear and murder into any land. Or maybe there was need for some fear, enough to command respect so that he could live on his land in peace. But he still believed that there might be other and more effective ways to command respect. He simply hadn't found them.

Two more times he snaked out the gun. In spite of his familiarity with firearms, this rhythm would not have occurred to him. But because of it, in little more than a week he could already do what Lashner wanted him to do. He could have whipped out the gun in his sleep, never doubting that his fingers and thumb would fall exactly into place.

He slid the revolver into his holster, patted it once, and felt the heavy sting of a rawhide rope as it encircled his body and snapped shut, pinning his arms to his sides. Someone yelled, the dun bolted, and the taut rope snapped him from the saddle.

The trees seemed to rise into the air. He hit the ground kicking, but his body was dragging over brush and hard ground before he fully realized what was happening. When the movement stopped his gun was pulled from its holster, and the butt slammed twice into his temple before he could free himself. Fire shot into his head and the trees tilted crazily. He raised his hand to ward off the next blow, but he was not prepared for the hard fingers that clenched him under the armpits and muscled him to his feet.

The rope slipped free. He struck out feebly with what little strength remained in him and a smashing blow landed on his cheekbone. As the ground flew up to him again he was kicked repeatedly in the ribs. He caught hold of the boot and clung to it and was pummeled with rough hands.

He felt himself being dragged to his feet again, and this time his arms were pinned behind him and his weak legs were unable to do more than feel desperately for balance. More blows rained against his belly, his chest, his face, and his head rolled like a balloon on a stick.

When the pummeling stopped, a twangy voice wheezed into his ear, 'We've got a message for you, Langston. Somethin' you'll be glad to hear.' It was several seconds before Derek's mind cleared enough to be sure that it was Griff who held him.

'That is right,' Cervantes' soft voice cut in. 'You will be very glad. What we wish to say is, we are not going to kill you, señor.'

'That's right, we're not,' Griff said. 'We're

113

not, because we want you to fix up that ranch and gather up those cattle. But after that, mister, your life's not worth a plugged centavo.'

Derek's mind was working now, but it was useless to try to move. Griff's heavy weight still pinioned his arms, and in front of him he could see the gleam of moonlight shining against Cervantes' gun.

'All right,' Griff wheezed. 'Put that gun away and do what you're supposed to do. He won't fight back; he's too weak to shake off a sandflea.'

Cervantes holstered the gun and stepped forward and lashed out with a right to Derek's belly. Pain shot up into his chest and down into his groin.

But Griff grated, 'Damn it, hit him in the face! Mark him up!'

Derek struggled now to fling Griff off; he forced the man sideways and was able to turn, but Cervantes circled with him, his small fists lashing out like bone-jarring streaks of flame.

In the midst of his struggling Griff let go suddenly and Derek sank to the ground. He rolled over, tried to rise and couldn't.

'It is finished,' Cervantes said. 'But do not forget. You are safe now. You are safe now because you work for us.'

Somehow they weren't there any more. Maybe he had been unconscious for a while, but he was alone now, lying on his belly in a patch of moonlight, with only the night sounds to keep him company.

He struggled to his feet, staggering and weaving to gain his balance. After a moment the uncertain earth settled and he saw the dun tied firmly to a springy bush only a short distance away. Even his gun was there on the ground beside the horse.

Why the hell had they done it? he wondered dully. It wasn't just for revenge. *Mark him up*, Griff had said. He ran his hand up over his bruised face; his upper lip was already beginning to puff and one eye was rapidly swelling shut. His cheek was over-sized and numb and he had to feel of his nose several times to make certain that it was not broken. The corner of his mouth was split and he wiped away a steady trickle of blood that flowed from it.

He moved up to the horse and it seemed that his whole head swelled as he bent to retrieve the gun. He brushed loose debris from the weapon and holstered it. The dun shied and snorted as he reached for the reins and he tried to speak calmly to it. But he was forced to keep his teeth together, and the sounds came out slurring and mushy. His ribs hurt as he mounted, but his face was worse—far worse—than his body. It seemed numb and frozen and at the same time painful as a bee sting. And it made no sense—less sense even than the fight he'd had with Otis at

115

the boot shop. But there'd been a reason for it, and when the time came he'd know what it was.

He kept his teeth together and clucked, and the dun started toward the ranch house.

* * *

The house was silhouetted darkly against the moonlight, its fieldstone chimney looking tall and sentry-like over the three-foot-high walls.

There'd be some fuss made, Derek reflected, if the men woke up. He tried to be quiet as he corralled the dun and walked up behind the house to the crude wooden bench that always held a bucket of water and a tin basin.

But no one would ever be quiet enough for Lashner. He rose over the waist-high walls, gun drawn and ready. Derek had been prepared for a strong reaction from the man, but still he was surprised at the almost hysterical high-pitched quality in his voice.

'What the hell happened to you?'

Derek bent over the washpan and gingerly began dabbing his eyes. 'It was Griff and Cervantes, waiting in the brush.' His words were still slurred. 'Cervantes roped me and Griff hit me with a gun butt. It's hard to be sure what happened after that.'

Lashner's wrath exploded so violently that Otis, Jackson and Ridge all scrambled up and

116

came to stand beside him. 'Damn it!' he raged. 'I told you you shouldn't go alone! That's what the hell I'm here for!' His left thumb gouged under his belt and began furiously to massage his belly.

Derek patted his swollen face with a dry handkerchief. 'That's not what you're here for,' he corrected. 'You're here as an instructor. Nothing else.'

'That ain't what everybody figgers,' Lashner said hotly. 'They figger I'm here to keep this from happenin' to you. And now they'll figger I couldn't do it. By God! You get back on your horse and lead us to the spot where it happened! We'll start trackin' 'em right now in the moonlight, and come daylight we'll run 'em down. By God! They'll hurt a while before we string 'em up, I can tell you that!'

'They won't hurt because we're not going after them,' Derek said coldly.

'What the hell you mean—not goin' after 'em? You mean you don't give a damn if everybody comes along and beats hell out of you like this?'

'I mean that there's no law to take them off our hands. And I can't go find somebody and murder them in cold blood, and that's what it would amount to. Besides, I've got to have a herd on the trail in less than six weeks, and I need every bit of that time.'

'There's things more important than cattle

drives!'

'Not to me. I've got one chance and I'm not going to lose it. Tomorrow we'll start branding cattle, so I'll have no trouble on that score. Some of the cattle here are five years old—maybe older—and have never had a brand on them. And we'll lose a lot of them soon if they're not branded.'

Lashner snorted. 'Hell, you might as well give all of 'em away. You cain't keep 'em nohow if you won't fight.'

'That's my worry, not yours.'

'The hell you say. I got a reputation to keep and everybody knows I'm working for you and I cain't afford for nothin' like this to happen.'

'Then you just tell everybody why I hired you. It's as simple as that! Now all of you can go back to bed—I don't feel like arguing any more.'

The others complied, but Lashner stood in his tracks while Derek went around to the doorway and crawled between the blankets. He reached down and slid his boots off; the rest of his clothes were ripped and torn, anyway. It was the last outfit of dress clothes he had, but he didn't feel like trying to salvage any of it. Not tonight. He was bone-weary and bruised all over.

He dropped off into a deep sleep, but the impression remained that Lashner in his fury was still standing.

118

Derek awoke with a swollen, aching head, and opened his eyes to see Otis crouched down in front of the fireplace frying bacon. The smell made him nauseous and the sight of Otis' foreboding face didn't help.

'What's on your mind, Sam?'

'Did you know Lashner lit out last night?'

Derek sat up and was instantly sorry and cradled his head in his hands. 'Bedroll and all?'

'Yep.'

Otis handed him a steaming cup of coffee and after a few swallows he began to feel better. 'I guess he couldn't stand it that I wouldn't go after Griff and Cervantes.'

Otis nodded, then looked at Derek speculatively. 'Stirrin' up a gunman's like proddin' a polecat. You never get by with just a little stink. But I'd say you come out lucky. Mostly a killer's a lot harder to fire than he is to hire.'

Derek stood up and started peeling off the ruins of his clothes. 'I guess you're right,' he said soberly. 'But he did teach me a lot.'

'I sure hope he did 'cause you're goin' to have to be twicet as good as you would've if he'd never come along.'

'Meaning?'

'Well, folks think of you now as a mean one. Somebody who'll hire a gunman. Won't nobody believe you just took him on to teach you to shoot, if you know what I mean.'

119

Derek pulled on his jeans and buttoned them reflectively. 'Well, I'm sorry it happened like this, but I can't worry about it now. I've got too many other things on my mind. When I was in Centro I made arrangements with Saltner to hire some men—four if he can get them. They should be here in a day or two. Now you'd better send either Ridge or Jackson to ask Saltner to find three more for me. He knows everyone in that part of the country and he knows what they can do and what they can't. Tell him I'm paying top wages. I don't want killers, but I do want men who can fight and who will fight if they have to.'

'You figgerin' on Lashner coming back and startin' somethin'?'

'Why should he come back here? No, we're going to brand cattle on the Strip and if anyone tries to stop us, we'll fight.'

Otis licked his lips. 'I figgered you and Delphine Judson'd get everythin' all ironed out last night.'

Derek picked up a can of lard, pried the lid off and ran his finger inside. 'We did get everything straightened out,' he said finally. 'She wants the Strip and everything on it and so do I.' He began to smear the soothing grease on his face.

'I don't reckon I understand what you got in mind,' Otis said. 'You're hirin' three men to fight Delphine Judson, but you ain't
120

figgerin' on doin' nothin' about Griff and Cervantes. And you ain't worried about Lashner.'

Derek got up, put on his hat and buckled on his gun. 'I haven't forgotten about any of them. But the time to fight Delphine is now. And the time to fight Griff and Cervantes is later on, when they try to do something again. Next time I'll be expecting them. And if Lashner doesn't make a play soon, I'll even be ready for him. By then I'll have a dozen men—men who'll be willing to fight.'

Otis winced and his jaw set but he said nothing.

'All right,' Derek said. 'Get your man started and tell him to order three wagonloads of lumber while he's there. We can't expect a whole crew to sleep outside forever.'

'Yeah,' Otis said. 'I'll go along with that.'

'Then tell him, so you and I can get started. I'm going to have the Tower brand on every damned animal that even sets foot on this ranch!'

'Wait a minute,' Otis said. 'Looky there.' A man was riding out of the brush toward them and Otis' face suddenly lit up with recognition. 'Damn if it's not Billy Cedar!' He cupped his hand and yelled, 'Hey, Billy!' To Derek he said excitedly, 'Maybe he's talked some sense into Delphine.'

Otis ran out, and Derek followed more slowly. Cedar dismounted and waited for him, and as he came close Otis said, 'This here's Billy Cedar.'

Derek shook the hand of the lean, gray, middle-aged man. 'Come on to the ranch house and have some coffee.'

Otis was like a schoolboy. 'I'll corral your horse, Billy. Then I got to go find Jackson and send him to Centro.'

'Thanks.' Cedar handed him the reins and he and Derek walked slowly toward the doorway. 'I've seen you a time or two,' Cedar said hesitantly. 'I don't guess you remember me.'

'I remember you. I saw you with Delphine twice. Once you watched me fighting Sam Otis and the second time you tried to save my guns.'

Cedar shrugged. 'What's done is done. But it might not be too late for some things, and I might as well come straight to the point. I've come here to talk about the Strip.'

Derek led the way to the fireplace and hunkered down beside it. He poured two battered tin cups full of steaming coffee and handed one to Cedar. He was forced to sip his from one corner of his bruised mouth, but Cedar studiously appeared not to notice.

'Delphine and I talked about the Strip last night,' Derek said. 'We didn't agree.'

'I know.' Cedar noisily sipped his own coffee. 'I wish I could say she sent me because she's changed her mind. But she

122

didn't—change her mind or send me, neither one.'

'Then I don't see what we can talk about.'

'That's what Delphine said this morning when I tried to reason with her.' Cedar looked squarely at Derek. 'I've never seen her so boilin' mad! But she did tell me some things about you that made me think you might listen.'

'Such as?'

'She said you was in a war, too. Said you'd been a soldier for years and that you'd fought in that cavalry charge against the Russians. So I figgered maybe you felt the same way I did about killin' when there wasn't no use in it.'

'I'd think, being raised in this country, you'd know there was a need for it sometimes,' Derek argued.

Cedar put down his cup and nestled his right wrist in his left hand. 'That's maybe true, but there won't always be a need for it. Some day they'll decide in Washington whether we're citizens or not, now that the war is over. They'll get the Yankee soldiers out an' our courts'll start operatin' again and more people'll come into this country. Then we'll settle ever'-thing the way we ought to.'

'The way I see it,' Derek answered, 'what's going to happen in the future has nothing to do with Delphine and me and the Strip.'

'Well, that ain't the way I see it,' Cedar said stubbornly. 'Figger it like this—you got more'n enough cattle right here—more'n you can take care of in the next year, maybe longer. An' anything Delphine takes, she's goin' to have to pay back when you go to court. In the meantime maybe she'll even come to her senses. What I'm tryin' to do is dodge a fight, gettin' people killed when there ain't any use in it.'

'Then I'd say you and Sam ought to go into partnership!'

Cedar shook his head. 'I reckon Sam and I don't feel the same about fightin'. I went on Delphine's third cattle drive and he didn't. I fought, too, when there was a need for it, and I'll do it again. And I'll tell you somethin' about Sam—he'll fight too, if he has to. He's just got a different idee of what a man ought to fight for.'

Derek rinsed out his cup and put it aside and Cedar did the same. 'Maybe I'd be willing to do it the way you want to,' Derek said. 'But I'd lose face in this country and I can't afford that. And I'll tell you another thing—the day I came here I'd have done it with no argument. Maybe I can blame it on the country or maybe on what's happened to me here. But I don't feel like settling things peacefully any more. I feel like drawing a line and standing on one side of it and daring anyone else to cross over to my side.'

Cedar stood up. 'People get like that here,' he conceded. 'Maybe I was like that once and—I don't know—maybe I still am. Maybe I was hopin' for more from you than I'd be willin' to give. And maybe I'm doin' the same with Delphine. She was always pretty much like a daughter to me, though we ain't been so close since I come back. But I'll tell you what I'll do for the next hour or two while you're thinkin' it over—I reckon no matter how much you know about some kinds of cattle, there ain't no man knows enough about longhorns less'n he's lived with 'em for years. And I see Otis and Ridge out poppin' brush, so I figger you're gettin' ready to start brandin'.'

Derek nodded. 'And next week we'll be branding on the Strip.'

'Well, wherever you do it,' Cedar said, 'it's a good thing to work in pairs. And if you want I'll work with you for the next couple of hours. I've got a sort of curiosity anyway that don't never get satisfied. I reckon the truth is, I'd like to hear more about these wars you fought in and sort of compare 'em with the one I fought.'

In spite of his puffed lips Derek grinned. 'There are a few things I'd like to learn, too. About handling cattle. About your war. About the drives. About the people here, and a lot of other things.'

Cedar grinned back. 'All right, then,' he said. 'We'll talk each other's ears off while we're tryin' to get our breath from rasslin' cattle.'

'And I'll do this much,' Derek said. 'I'll think about staying off the Strip for a time, and I'll think about it hard.'

He started to the corral to get the horses and found himself whistling between his teeth, and he couldn't help wondering at the change one reasonable man could bring about. Hell, maybe even Delphine would soften up one of these days. After all, he was simply asking for his own property, and for the right to live on it and take his cattle to market. Maybe she wouldn't feel that was too much if she thought it over.

CHAPTER ELEVEN

With six of her crew riding at her back, Delphine Judson arrived in La Partida in midafternoon and tied up in front of the bank. There was a bar at the other end of town and she knew the men would want a few drinks, but now they obediently sat their horses while she went inside. In spite of Billy Cedar's warning, they'd go only when she gave the word and that wouldn't be until her business with Willetts was finished and done with.

Willetts was sitting motionless at his desk like a round-faced inscrutable Oriental, but

126

when she came in he hurriedly pushed his spectacles into place and started ponderously to get up.

'Sit still,' Delphine snapped.

'Well, now, Miss Delphine,' Willetts said, 'if you don't mind I guess that's just what I will do. I'm glad you dropped by, though. I haven't seen you for a while.'

She ignored his overtures toward friendship and said coolly, 'How much money do you have in this bank?'

'Why, I reckon I've got all I need. You fixin' to draw some out?' He slid pen and paper toward her. 'You just say how much you want and sign right here.'

'When I get ready to draw some out I'll tell you. What I want to know right now is—how much money do you have in this bank? To the exact penny.'

His brow wrinkled with sudden worry. 'Why, I guess—countin' everythin', maybe nine thousand dollars.'

'You've got nine thousand cash in the bank? This minute?'

'Well, maybe not all here right this minute.'

She planted both hands flat on the desk and bent over close to him. 'Mr. Willetts,' she said, 'I don't have very much patience today. I'm going to ask you once again, and if you don't give me an exact answer I'm going to bring six men into this bank and tear it apart.

Then I'm going to put you on a horse and ride you out of town and make damn sure you never come back. Now. How much money do you have in this bank? This minute! To the exact cent!' She straightened up, folded her arms and stood waiting.

He took a breath as though to argue some more, looked once into her eyes, then pushed the creaking chair back and got up. He began to scrabble ponderously through several books on a shelf along the wall, dragged one out, brushed it off, and sat heavily back down to open it. He looked again at Delphine, sitting now manlike on a corner of his desk, swinging her booted leg up and down; she seemed small and gentle and defenseless until he saw her face; then he hurriedly began jotting figures from the book onto a piece of paper. After several minutes of hasty figuring, he drew one broad line and put a number under it.

'In the bank right this minute,' he said, 'I got seven thousand, three hundred and forty-four dollars and twelve cents.'

Delphine smiled. She stood up and picked up the pen and the little pad of receipts. 'Six thousand of that is mine. I want it—now!' Her pen scratched busily.

Willetts squirmed. 'Well, sure, Miss Delphine. But you hadn't ought to take out that much at once. Somebody's liable to knock you in the head for it.'

'That shouldn't concern you,' she said, handing him the paper. 'I'll have my money. Now.'

He got up again and this time his legs seemed weaker, almost unable to support his heavy body. He went back to the curtain, parted it and opened the heavy lock on the safe. When the door swung open, he unlocked a metal box and drew money from it. He moved nervously back to the desk, put the money in front of her and began slowly to count aloud.

'Six thousand and forty-four dollars even,' he said finally, and slowly pulled back his pudgy hands, letting his fingers rest on the edge of the desk. 'But, Miss Delphine,' he looked up at her pleadingly, 'I'd rather you didn't mention this. You know how hard times are. I've had to loan out ever' cent I could. Anytime there's a chance in hell a man could pay me back I've been lendin' him money. Somebody's got to do that, Miss Delphine. That's the only way this country'll get in any kind of shape.'

'I tried to borrow money from you during the war,' she said coldly. 'And you didn't lend it to me.' She picked up the money and began stuffing it in her pockets.

'No, ma'am, I didn't,' Willetts defended. 'An' I told you why at the time. Confed'rate money wasn't worth nothin' then, and what little gold I had was just a shoestring—and it had to go where it'd do the most good. I did say I'd lend you enough to buy any groceries you needed; I couldn't afford nothin' else. But you wasn't satisfied with that. You had some big idee about buildin' up your ranch right in the middle of the war.'

'I asked you for money and you didn't give it to me. That's all that matters. And before this day's over there'll be other people asking you for money and you won't give it to them either, because you won't have it.'

Willetts recoiled. 'What do you mean by that?'

She smiled. 'I mean you're going to keep this bank open while I tell everybody else that there won't be enough money for them if Derek Langston takes his. And you're going to give them their money when they ask for it. When he comes there won't be any.'

Willetts stiffened and grew resolute. 'No, ma'am. I ain't doin' any such thing. I'm shuttin' this bank down until I can talk sense into ever'body. I'm short on money because I got faith in the people around here. They got to have faith in me, too. Faith in my judgment. An' I want ever'body who ever put a nickel in here to get it back, includin' Langston.'

Delphine was still smiling. 'If you don't do it the way I want you to, then I'll send word to him that you haven't enough money to pay him. And he'll come and draw his. Then

130

some of the people around here won't get any. Why there must be fifty people entitled to some of what you have left. If you fail half of them you'll have to leave town and never come back. But if you fail just Langston you'll have enough for everybody else. And you can open up again when he's gone.'

'I don't have enough anyway,' he argued. 'All I've got left is thirteen hundred dollars, and I'm supposed to have twenty-five hundred, not countin' three hundred of my own.'

'Then I'll give you back two hundred. I'll lose that much, you'll lose your three hundred, and Langston will lose his thousand. Everybody else will get theirs.' She counted out the money.

'I won't do it,' he said stubbornly.

'You've got no choice.' She turned and called through the door, 'You men scatter out and spread the word. Anybody who wants their money will have to get here before Derek Langston does. If he gets his there won't be enough for anybody else.'

'I cain't let it happen,' Willetts pleaded. 'I got to close up—right now.'

'Gort,' Delphine called, 'you stay here with Mr. Willetts. If he tries to close up, you know what to do. And after the last penny's drawn out I want you to ride to the Tower Ranch and tell Derek Langston what happened.'

She saw the cowboy grin, and knew that

Gort would take care of everything.

CHAPTER TWELVE

The constant coming and going of the bank depositors during the rest of the day let Griff, Cervantes and Lashner ride in at sunset unnoticed. The general store held no customers when they pulled up in front of it. Hees saw them through the window, rushed over to the door and ushered them inside. He quickly locked the door behind them. His eyes were filled with excitement and triumph as he pulled down the shades and spun about in the semi-darkness.

'Well?'

Cervantes grinned. 'You are a smart one, señor. Langston did not wish to come after us. He does not like to kill, just as you said. But also, just as you said, the Señor Lashner did come. We were waiting, hidden, and when he came past us we held rifles on him until we were able to speak—to tell him what we wanted.'

The corner of Lashner's mouth lifted and his eyes narrowed as he glared hard at Cervantes. 'You better not spend too much time tellin' about you holdin' a rifle in my back!'

Hees quickly spread both hands, palms

out. 'We'll have no fightin' amongst ourselves,' he ordered crisply. He looked at Lashner and this time there was no fear on his face. 'The fact that you're here means you want in for a cut of what we're about to make. An' it means somethin' else and you may's well get it straight right now—I'm the one givin' the orders!' He pointed to each in turn, 'To Griff—Cervantes—and to you. You just do like I say and we'll all make money. You run around throwin' tantrums and you'll wind up with nothin'.'

Griff continued leaning against the door-jamb, and Cervantes' grin remained fixed on his mouth. But Lashner's face tightened. He locked eyes with Hees and scowled until the silence grew thick. But after a moment went by without action, Hees felt his own position grow stronger. He continued smoothly, 'All right, then. That part of it's settled. We need you and you need us. But it ain't just a matter of cattle. I got a store needs savin'.'

Lashner's thumb began to massage his belly and his fingers spread fanwise. 'The hell with the store,' he gritted. 'I got a reputation to save, an' I ain't doin' it here in town. We got to settle somethin' damn fast. If you make it worth my while to work for you, then the first thing I'll do is kill the Englishman. If you don't make it worth my while then I'm still workin' for him, so I'll kill you.'

133

Hees's wide mouth spread thin. 'You're the one better get things straight,' he said. 'You ain't bluffin' me—not now nor any other time. You want to shoot, you do it. You want to shut up and listen, you do that too.'

Again the two sets of eyes locked and again Hees spoke as if there had been no interruption. 'As I was sayin', I got a business to save. This feller Saltner'll be sendin' another wagon load of stuff tomorrer mornin'. I cain't stop him from comin' here; I couldn't if I had a dozen men like you. He's big and he's powerful and he sends shotgun guards. If we killed one of 'em, like as not he'd send fifty next time. But there's one thing I can do—and you're the one to tend to it.'

'Are you forgettin' about the Englishman?' Lashner demanded.

'No, but you can,' Hees said, 'till the right time comes. Today I want the three of you to make the rounds. I want ever'body in and out of town to know you'll be right here tomorrer when Saltner's wagons come. I want 'em to know, that you ain't goin' to like it, neither. So after them wagons are gone you'll pay a visit to anybody that spends one red cent with Saltner.'

Griff spread both feet and set his solid jaw. 'What about Langston? And what about the cattle? We're not sharin' in your business.'

Hees turned on him savagely. 'If they

134

freeze me outa business I won't have one dime to finance a cattle drive—not even enough for beans.' He relaxed a little and grinned at the three men. 'Besides, we don't have to worry about Langston. Delphine Judson's started in on him already—and we'll finish up.'

Cervantes' interest quickened and his eyes fairly gleamed. 'The last time you depended on the señorita, Saltner's wagons came.'

'This time it's different!' Hees walked over and raised the door shade slightly, looking out at the crowded street. 'By nightfall he'll be broke exceptin' what money he's got in his pocket. An' after tomorrer, when nobody buys from Saltner, his wagons won't be comin' back. That means Langston's got to go a long ways for supplies he cain't pay for, and he's got to hire men on nothin' but promises and that's gettin' old around here.'

Hees slapped a particle off his bald head and pulled the shade back down. He paced heavily in front of the others, dry-washing his hands. 'Now! There's four men due here from Centro to work for Langston. You, Lashner, tell 'em Langston cain't pay, and besides that you don't want 'em here. I've got a notion they'll go back.'

Cervantes walked lightly over to the counter and hoisted himself up backwards. 'And the Señor Langston?' he demanded. 'What will he do about all this?'

'There ain't but one thing he can do,' Hees said, 'short of just givin' up and goin' away. Ever'body knows ol' Corenson's fixin' to make an early drive. It's a damn fool thing, but Langston'll have to gather up what cattle he can, with what crew he can get, and beat it up north to join him. And that don't give him more'n two weeks, and it's at least seven days drivin' time. If he comes to town in the meantime, Lashner'll kill him. If he don't, we'll let him gather up a herd, an' then we'll take it.'

Cervantes banged his boot heels against the counter and scowled, shaking his head. 'Then it is we who will be fools to make an early drive.'

Hees went over to the windows and started slowly letting up the shades. As the light flooded into the store he shook his head, his face set with satisfaction. 'We ain't makin' no drive,' he said. 'Leastwise not a long one. The river's high now and we're heading for it. We'll send a load of hides and salt beef down the Rio Grande and acrost the Gulf to New Orleans. There's less profit that way, but it's better'n nothin'.'

Griff said hoarsely, 'Maybe Langston'll think of doin' that.'

'He don't even have the money to pay shippin' fees,' Hees said. 'An' I told you I'd do the worryin'. Now you three get goin'. An' don't you overlook nobody. I don't want one

136

single person to even walk up to Saltner's wagons.'

CHAPTER THIRTEEN

Sara Otis awoke with mingled feelings of anticipation and dread. All week long she'd been so nervous waitin' for this day she'd hardly been able to stand it, because Sam had said that today she could buy enough calico from Saltner to make herself a dress, and enough extra to make Robert a shirt.

But yesterday awful things had happened. To start with, that terrible Judson girl had caused Derek Langston to lose all his money. Maybe he had some left, but a man didn't carry much around in his pocket, not in this country.

She'd been worried about that just before dark. Then the cold-eyed killer, Rig Lashner, had paid her a visit, and it didn't seem worth worryin' about no more. He wouldn't ever come back to visit her, he said, less'n she bought somethin' off Saltner's wagon this mornin'.

She scolded herself for lying in bed after she was awake. It was somethin' she hadn't done in years. Well, then, she wouldn't do it now. She crawled from beneath the ragged blankets and hastily dragged her clothes on.

137

She yelled, 'Robert! Robert, you get out of that bed!'

She brushed her hair from her eyes and headed for the tin wash pan on the bench outside, her face hardening with resolve. Nobody'd told her what to do for a long time, now. Nobody 'cept Sam, and he didn't count, bein' so reasonable and all.

No, that wasn't the reason he didn't count. He didn't count because he was so much a part of her they didn't seem like two people no more. They had memories together that nothin' could ever break. Memories of Tim, for instance. He'd been three when he died. Sam was off fightin' the war at the time, and they both knew if he hadn't been gone the kid might've lived. But they both knew, too, that his goin' had been her idea just as much as his.

She didn't rightly know any more just why she'd flared up against the Yankees the way she had. But it seemed like all the other women had been the same—maybe even worse'n the men. In their minds they'd pictured their husbands ridin' into battle wavin' their swords, and they'd seen the enemy breakin' and runnin' in all directions. And they'd pictured their men comin' home in bright clean uniforms with all kinds of ideas about how to make a new nation great. But it hadn't happened like that. Instead, they'd come back starvin' and beaten, and they were still starvin'.

The water in the wash pan was cold and it helped to wake her up some. She yelled back in the house, 'Robert! I ain't goin' to tell you again!' She was bein' too hard on the boy, she thought. He didn't loaf around all the time like most of the other kids in town. He tended the little garden, watched after the chickens and gathered up the eggs and even helped her in the house sometimes. He was a good kid, the best there ever was, she reckoned.

She went back into the kitchen, met Robert and hastily shooed him out toward the wash pan.

'An' you gather up some wood first thing after breakfast,' she yelled.

She kindled a fire in the old iron stove and carefully measured out a small portion of grits. She wasn't goin' to do it, she decided fiercely. She wasn't goin' to let Hees tell her what to do. It was a free country and she'd do just like she pleased and there wasn't nothin' Hees could do about it when it came right down to it. Maybe her husband wasn't here, but this town was full of growed men and they weren't goin' to let things happen to the women and the kids. An' you couldn't go around lettin' all the Heeses run this world.

She clanked the battered frying pan solidly onto the stove. There she went, thinkin' all kinds of things that maybe shouldn't even enter her mind. Maybe she wasn't worried about standin' up and doin' what was right; maybe she was just thinkin' about how bad she wanted that calico.

When Robert came back in she said gently, 'You got to so some weedin' in the garden today. But you gather up the wood first and then the eggs. And after that I don't want you to leave the house. I want you right here where I can look after you all day.'

Robert said, 'Aw gee, Ma, cain't I even go to the wagons with you?'

'No, you cain't,' she snapped. 'You mind what I say or I'll tan your hide till it's blistered for a month! Now shoo!'

★   ★   ★

It was midmorning when Sara threw the thin shawl over her shoulders and resolutely started for the center of town. The sun was up high now, warming the air some, and the sky was almost cloudless. She clamped her jaw; she'd heard the wagons rumble into town about ten minutes ago, but she didn't hear any noise now like she'd heard this time last week an' the week before that. She didn't hear people yellin' and laughin' like it was carnival time in Santone; in fact, now that she thought about it, she hadn't even heard any of the usual Saturday morning sounds.

She turned onto the street and there were

the wagons sure enough, the two drivers standing up on the seats, the canvas tops thrown back to display their merchandise, and the two shotgun guards sitting their horses off to one side. But there weren't any customers.

Her glance swept slowly around the town and she saw a few heads peeking from around buildings, a dozen men scattered along the boardwalks, and Rig Lashner leaning idly against a post in front of Hees's store. The sunny day became cold and she could feel goose bumps rise all over her; he hadn't been bluffin', then. Hadn't been bluffin' about watchin', and likely hadn't been bluffin' about payin' a visit afterwards to anybody who bought from the wagons.

She squared her shoulders; she was goin' to go over to the wagons and buy—her lips trembled—and buy a ready-made shirt for Robert. She wouldn't buy the calico; that way he'd know she wasn't doin' it just for herself. And afterwards when Rig Lashner came around she'd point the old muzzle-loading rifle at his belly, and she'd pull the trigger, too, if he tried anything funny. Hees had made her life a hell on earth for long enough, and Saltner and his outfit had been nicer than any man had any need to be. She'd be lettin' this whole part of the country down if she didn't go over there and buy somethin'.

She heard a little swell of voices as she

141

angled across the street toward the wagons. Even Lashner straightened up for a moment, but before she'd taken three steps, he slumped back against the post. A hush fell over the street.

As she neared the wagon the driver shot a glance toward Lashner, then looked down at her and grinned. 'Howdy, ma'am. Looks like you're the only one in this town that ain't short on nerve. What you aimin' to buy? You name it and I'll dig it out.'

She pushed up against the wagon side and looked longingly between the staves at all the merchandise before she said slowly, 'I want a shirt for my boy Robert. He's nine.'

The driver crawled back into the wagon. 'A shirt? You betcha—and anythin' else you want, too. Your credit's better'n anybody else's in this town.'

'Just a shirt,' she snapped. 'I don't buy on credit. Not no more I don't!'

The driver rummaged through a pile of dry goods and produced a red-and-black plaid wool shirt. 'I reckon for an average boy of nine this here ought to do the job,' he said.

She licked her lips and said harshly, 'It'll have to be smaller. He ain't average size.'

'Smaller it is, then,' he said. He quickly produced another shirt. 'This here's bound to do it. Now how about something for yourself?'

'Nope. This shirt'll do it. How much?'

The driver's back was still to her. When he turned he was holding a bolt of calico, prettier'n anything she'd ever dreamed of. 'You mean to say you couldn't use a few yards of pretty material like this?'

She dug into a pocket with a shaking hand and held out a coin to him. 'You just say how much that shirt is. I ain't buyin' nothin' else.'

Instead of taking the coin he began to unroll cloth from the bolt and when he ripped it there must've been enough goods in his hands to make two dresses and two shirts and maybe even more. He folded it carefully and held it out to her. 'Ma'am, you consider this a present from Saltner and Brother.'

'I don't want no present. I've took charity sometimes, but not for myself!'

He looked astonished. 'Why, I guess you don't understand, ma'am. This here's not charity. This here is Saltner's way of sayin' he treats folks right. If you don't take this right out here where everybody can see it, why, you're doin' us a big disservice. When's the last time ol' Hees over there ever give anything away?' He shook his head again, thrusting the material at her. 'No, ma'am, there's no charity connected with this. We've got to show folks there's nothin' to be scared of. You've did your part and now we're doin' ours. And you just forget about payin' for that shirt, too. I reckon we're plumb even.'

She took the material and clutched it in

143

both hands. She tried to say, 'Thanks,' but she was too choked up and the word wouldn't come out. She turned hurriedly away and started back across the street, her eyes streaming until she could hardly see.

But Lashner was already moving to cut her off and by the time she reached the boardwalk he had drawn up even with her. He blocked her way and she stopped rigidly.

Lashner grinned. 'You're a hard-headed ol' woman, ain't you? But you didn't do no good for yourself nor nobody else by goin' out there to that wagon. I said I'd be by to see you and I'm sayin' it again.'

She found her voice and said, 'You'll get a bullet for your trouble!' She went around him and marched stiffly on toward the house.

Lashner stood helplessly in his tracks, for one of the few times in his life uncertain about what he should do. Damfool woman! If she'd been a man he'd have put a bullet in the small of her back and that would have been the end of it! But you couldn't shoot a woman in the back. Hell, why was he worried anyhow? This was Hees's business. He looked down the street and saw the boardwalk loungers begin to slink away. He snorted. At a time like this, he'd hoped some of the others would take nerve from the old woman and try to start something. Once they did that he'd know exactly what to do. His lips curled in disgust. They wouldn't start anything. There wasn't enough guts in the lot of them to fill up a chicken's belly. He went on back to the store, enjoying the sight of the big grown men disappearing before him.

Inside, he hooked his thumbs in his gun belt and said, 'Well, you seen what happened.'

Hees was across the counter, his round face red with anger. 'I seen it and I aim to do somethin' about it.'

Lashner said curiously, 'You figgerin' on me killin' that ol' woman?'

Hees shook his head. 'Nope. We ain't killin' nobody. It's simpler than that. We're just takin' her kid is all, and holding him till her and her ol' man moves out of town. I reckon by tomorrer they'll be gone, and nobody else'll know what happened. They'll just know to keep away from them wagons.'

'What'll you do with the kid?'

'Nothin',' Hees said. 'Nothin' at all, if they do like I say.'

*   *   *

It was late afternoon when Sara Otis poked her head out the kitchen window to make another check on Robert. She hadn't wanted him outside at all any more today, but he'd insisted and it was true the garden needed to be weeded and anyway she'd kept her head out the window until she had a crick.

Her heart pounded once like a hammer blow. Inside the rickety little fence that enclosed the garden, she saw the hoe lying flat on the ground and Robert gone.

She rushed outside. 'Robert! Robert!' Then, frantically, 'Robert! You come here this minute!' Her hurried steps began to circle the house. Where could that fool kid be? The eggs were already gathered, the wood was in, and she'd told him he couldn't play with the other kids! Not today!

She peered into the brush beyond the weedy lot, trying to force him to appear in front of her like magic. But he wasn't there. She stood back to look up on the roof, then fell to her knees and looked under the sagging floor. Almost frantic, she circled the house again and cut off toward town at a fast trot. When she found him she'd feel foolish, likely, for not bothering to go back inside for her shawl; the day was growing colder by the minute. But right now she wouldn't have gone back if a norther started blowing down on her.

When she came to the street, it was bare and empty. She ran faster, stopping each time she came to a wide gap between two buildings, where Robert might be playing. But it seemed like none of the kids were out playing today. Gasping for breath, she ran down the walk, past Hees's store, past the saddle shop to an old empty hut that stood up

146

two feet off the ground on mesquite logs. Sometimes kids liked to play under a house like that.

She crawled on her hands and knees, squinting to see into the gloom. But Robert wasn't there, either, and she knew suddenly and with a terrible sickness that she wouldn't find him anywhere, not until after she'd talked to Casper Hees. She scrambled up and hurried back to the store, her heart beating wildly.

Hees and Lashner, leaning easily against the counter, were the only two people inside. She stopped in front of Hees, her breath coming in painful gasps, and blurted out, 'Have you—have you seen Robert?'

Hees's mouth spread in a malicious smile. 'Ain't it almighty late for you to be thinkin' about him?'

'What—what do you mean?'

He came round and stood in front of her, shaking a thick forefinger in her face. 'I mean just this—you keep your mouth shut, but you head out to that ranch and get your husband, and the two of you got till tomorrer noon to hightail it out of this town. You do, and you won't get more'n ten miles along the road and you'll have your kid back. You don't, you won't never get him back. And if you pop off to anybody else—you tell one single person 'sides Sam Otis, and Robert's life ain't worth two cents. Now you get! And you mind what

I told you about keepin' your mouth shut.'

The shock that set into Sara Otis kept her from moving at first. Her legs almost turned to water and she reeled. 'We'll—we'll go,' she said pleadingly. 'Give him to me now and we'll go. I'll go tonight and never come back.'

'We'll give him to you ten miles out of town,' Hees said, '—if you keep your lip buttoned. Otherwise you won't never see him again.' He pushed her toward the door. 'Tomorrer noon,' he reminded. 'We're goin' to be out on the road about two o'clock, but we won't wait long! You better just be there—you and Otis both.'

The street was a swimming blur before Sara Otis' eyes as she ran down the boardwalk, crying and wheezing for breath, and rushed blindly into the stable. When she could make out Harlan, busily forking hay into narrow stalls she rushed up to him and thrust a coin in front of her.

'I—I got to have a horse. Quick!' she cried.

He leaned on the fork as if it were a crutch and blinked solemnly at her. 'Why, Sary, now what would you want—'

'Quick!' She screamed it in his ear.

'Where you fixin' to go? These here horses are all I got and I cain't let nothin' happen to 'em.'

'I've got to see my husband right away.'

'All right, then.' He started hobbling toward the back. 'It must be pretty

148

important, the way you're carryin' on. I've got that old buggy out back. You can have that if you want.'

She was wringing her hands. 'All right—all right. But—please—please—please hurry.'

CHAPTER FOURTEEN

It was almost sunup on Sunday morning when Derek and Ridge reached the corral with their eight longhorns. Derek swore. This was where they'd have a hell of a time again. If only they had a third man to open the gate!

Derek tried to edge up to it on horseback, but a brindle steer bolted and was followed by three others before the gate swung open and it was all they could do to get the other four rolling-eyed creatures inside. That made twenty-eight they had altogether, and it was frustrating enough to make his belly churn until he wanted to heave.

He'd known Friday night that the end was near, when Gort had ridden up to tell him of the bank run. Still, he'd been left with some kind of hope that he could get up a herd and join Corenson. But Jackson was in Centro, Otis was laid up, gored from hip to knee after only two hours' work yesterday, and the cowboys Saltner was going to send hadn't arrived yet. Couple this with his own and

Ridge's ignorance concerning the handling of longhorns and the fact that they were short on time, and he'd have to admit that his chances rested more on hope than on anything he could point to.

Derek and Ridge both dismounted and muscled the rawhide-and-pole gate levers into place. Derek said, panting, 'I think we'd better throw up a partition across the corral. Then we could leave the gate open and we wouldn't lose so many after we got here with them.'

Ridge's face fell. Embarrassed, he said, 'I've seen plenty of 'em built like that. I don't know why I didn't think of it.' He started away. 'I'll get the tools, and we got a few posts left. It won't take long.'

They both heard the squeaking buggy at the same time, but Ridge called, 'Somebody's comin',' and pointed at the screen of brush to the east. 'Looks like Sary Otis! And she looks bad sick.'

As the buggy came closer they could see that she was reeling on the seat, almost unable to hold the reins. Both men started trotting to meet her.

The buggy lurched past them and Derek raced after it. He grabbed the reins and pulled the horse to a stop. At first Sara Otis appeared not to see either of them, but suddenly her eyes fastened on Derek. Lips trembling, she said, 'I—I been lost—I been lost all night. I—I got to see Sam—quick. Quick. I ain't got much time.'

He reached up and took her elbow. 'Here,' he said gently, 'I'll help you down. We'll walk the rest of the way and maybe you'll feel better.'

She jerked her arm free. 'No! No! I got to see Sam quick!'

Ridge said, 'Howdy, Sary,' and shifted uncomfortably from one foot to the other, not knowing what to do or say.

Derek climbed up and started to lift her down. He spoke quietly, but his words were clear and sharp. 'Ridge, take care of the horse, will you? Then come up to the house. I'll see if I can find out what's wrong.'

Ridge nodded and was already starting to unhitch the horse as Derek stepped down with Sara in his arms.

In spite of the load, Derek walked at a crisp pace until he was halfway to the house, when she seemed to straighten up some, and he was able to stop and put her down.

He remained close to her, careful not to let her fall, and said, 'Mrs. Otis, maybe you'd better tell me what the trouble is. Sam's hurt some. It's nothing serious, but he won't be able to work for a few days and it might be a month before he can ride.'

She almost fainted and he had to grab at her. 'No!' she moaned. 'No! No!'

He gripped both her shoulders and shook

151

her. 'You've got to straighten up!' he said. 'You can't worry Sam. Not when he's hurt already. But you tell me what the trouble is and I'll do what needs to be done.'

She fought him. 'I cain't tell!'

He said gently, 'You've got to tell somebody. And the way Sam feels, it might be best if you tell me.'

Her face took on a mask of resigned hopelessness and she stopped struggling and grew quiet. 'It's—it's—Robert.' She poured out the story between tight lips, and he felt hard knots come and go in his belly. He was sorry that the thought of saving his ranch even entered his mind, but he couldn't help thinking that he'd have to go to town now and that meant he'd lose the rest of the day and maybe tomorrow—at a time when every second was precious.

He said, 'Don't you worry about anything. I know how to deal with Hees.'

She moaned. 'No! No! He'll kill Robert!'

'I said I know what to do about it,' he said harshly. 'Now you come over to the house with me. You tell Sam you heard about him being hurt. Ridge told a passing cowboy and you were worried—that's why you came out here. Meanwhile, we'll hitch up the buggy with Sam's horse. Then you'll come back to town with us and we'll straighten up everything.'

Some of the fire came back into her then,

and she said accusingly, 'It's your doin'. If you hadn't've brought Lashner here this never would've happened!'

'All right, then,' he said wearily, 'it's my doing. But I'll tell you something—if you don't go to Sam and say just what I told you to say, and then come into town with us so your neighbors will believe us—the rest of it will be your doing!'

She winced and straightened up and he took her on to the doorway. 'You go inside now and don't you forget—all you're worried about is Sam's leg.'

He left her there and headed back to the corral with rapid strides. Ridge was just leading up the livery horse and Derek said crisply, 'Hobble him and turn him loose, then we'll catch Sam's horse and hitch him and head for town. Hees has Robert Otis.'

Ridge's face hardened and his fingers began to work with a fury. When the hobbles were in place the two of them mounted and galloped toward the grassy area where they were apt to find Ottis' hobbled bay.

'We've got to be in town by noon,' Derek grated as they pounded along. 'We'll have to do some hard riding!'

He told Ridge the story and watched his face darken. 'Hees must've gone plumb loco thinkin' he could get away with somethin' like that!'

They caught the bay easily, and riding back

153

Derek said, 'Lashner's working for Hees now.'

Ridge flung up his head. 'You mean—you mean—Lashner's got the kid?'

'Lashner and Hees together.'

'Then Robert might be dead by now.'

Derek shook his head. 'I don't think so. If Hees hurt him, then Otis would be like a madman. But as long as he isn't hurt, Otis would do anything Hees wanted him to. The way they figure is that the Otises will simply disappear after making a purchase from Saltner. No one will know where they went or why. Most people will think pretty hard before crossing Hees again.'

Ridge nodded. 'I guess you're right. But what'll we do about it?'

'I don't know yet. It depends on how soon we can get to town.' They reached the corral and dismounted. 'Hitch the bay, will you? I'll get Mrs. Otis.'

Ridge stood for a second, clearing his throat, his hand ruffling the bay's mane. 'You—you know—even if we get the breaks in town—you'll never be able to round up a herd after this. We was short on time anyway.'

Derek said, 'We'll talk about that when we get back!' and started rapidly away.

Within the low walls of the ranch house Otis lay on his back, his long face contorted with pain and at the same time reddened with anger. Sara Otis stood over him, her shoulders bent. At Derek's arrival, Otis snorted, 'Fool woman! She come off and left the kid in town with nobody to look after him!'

'I'll take her back,' Derek said. 'And I'll leave you food and water right by your bed here. Ridge is going to be busy—likely he won't have time to check in on you. And, Sam, don't you worry about anything. Everything's going to be all right. Or you, either, Mrs. Otis. Sam fought a war and came back, didn't he? A scratch like this won't keep him down for long.'

By the time he'd set a bucket of water nearby, along with a plate full of food scooped from two pots nestling on the dying coals in the fireplace, Mrs. Otis seemed to have recovered somewhat. He took her arm. 'Sam, I may be a little late getting back. You rest easy now!'

Otis nodded. 'You tell Robert he's not to let his ma worry about me again!'

Sara smiled stiffly as Derek led her from the ranch house, but when they were out of hearing, she shook her elbow loose from his hand. 'If that boy dies I ain't goin' to forgive nobody,' she said. 'Not me for takin' them goods, nor Sam for gettin' hisself hurt, nor you for bringin' Lashner and tryin' to ruin Hees.' She climbed into the buggy without help, but Ridge pushed her firmly aside on

155

the seat and took the reins.

'Sary,' he said gently, 'you cain't set there filled up with hate and fear and worry for another few hours. Not after the night you went through. You just try to lean on my shoulder and go to sleep. We'll be in town 'fore you know it.'

*   *   *

After nearly five hours of hard riding they reached the outskirts of La Partida. The pale sun was high overhead as Derek reined in the dun and leaned toward the buggy seat. 'Ridge, does Hees keep his store open on Sunday?'

Ridge nodded, and Sara Otis opened eyes that were sunken almost beyond belief. 'What you goin' to do?' she asked fearfully.

'First—which family do you know best here in La Partida?'

'The Graysons—they live behind Hees— building's acrost from the store.'

'Then we'll go there. Ridge, you lead the way, but don't ride past the store.'

Ridge clucked and the buggy creaked forward. The main street was almost deserted and over it lay the quiet air peculiar to Sunday in any village. If church bells had been tolling Derek could almost have imagined himself in England. But the quiet would be shattered soon, he thought, and if tears and soft crying came in the wake of the shattering, it would be because he had made a mistake. He saw with a relief he could not have believed that Lashner's beautiful brown stallion was still tied in front of the store and that the store was open.

They moved off the street and cut through a shallow gully. Ridge stopped the buggy in front of a small frame house with a yard full of half-withered flowers. Derek swung down. Sara Otis was whimpering again, her eyes stark with terror, her fists pounding her cheeks. 'What if they've taken him away? What if he's gone?'

Derek reached out and lifted her down. 'The store's open, Mrs. Otis, and Lashner's horse is there.'

'S'pose Robert's still in there then,' she moaned. 'S'pose they see us? They'll kill him! They'll kill him!'

'We'll do the best we can,' he promised.

She struggled out of his arms and stood poised for flight in front of the Graysons' gate. 'Best you can ain't good enough! Robert's got to be saved! He's got to be brought out of that store alive!'

Ridge came up and grabbed one arm and Derek took the other. They led her, struggling furiously, up the creaking steps to the front door.

The heavily-built woman who came to the doorway looked from Ridge to Derek with hostile astonishment. She stepped out and put her arms around Sara protectively. 'What's the trouble, Ben?'

Ridge pointed at Derek. 'This here's Mr. Langston—'

Derek interrupted, 'We don't have much time. Hees and Lashner have Robert Otis in their store. She's afraid they might kill him.'

Sara Otis was whimpering deep in her throat as Mrs. Grayson pulled her inside. 'You two come in here! Dan'll help you.'

Grayson had obviously heard them; his rocking chair was still moving gently, but he was out of it and leaning against the fireplace wrestling on his boots. 'Damn right I will,' he said. He was plump and breathing hard, his face beet red from the sudden exertion.

'Will the other men in town feel the same?'

Grayson brushed his hand over the shock of gray-black hair that jutted over his forehead. 'Just tell me what you want us to do,' he said simply.

'All right, then. You and Ridge go in different directions and round up at least a dozen men. Tell them to bring shotguns or rifles. I'll meet you in ten minutes at that shack'—he pointed—'just beyond the boot-shop. I'm going there now to keep a lookout.'

Grayson grabbed an old shotgun with twisted Damascus barrels from two pegs over the fireplace. 'Ten minutes it is. Ben, you get

Travers and the others over that way. I'll go north.'

As the three of them left, Derek heard the sound of cups being rattled in the kitchen behind them; woman's immemorial method of dealing with trouble, he thought.

The stallion was still at the hitching rail, and as Grayson and Ridge split off in opposite directions, Derek saw Lashner's face pressed to the store window. The gunman abruptly spun about and moved out of sight. That was good indication that the boy was still inside, Derek decided. If something hadn't been weighing on Lashner's mind, he'd have been out on the street already.

Derek reached the shack and stood impatiently, sliding the Remington up and down in its holster. He paced a few steps, looked at the rear store entrance, and came back to the street, wondering how the men would react when they were brought face to face with Lashner. The tall gunman could inspire fear in most people with only a glance because it was common knowledge that he wouldn't hesitate to kill, and wouldn't think about it afterwards. That alone was enough to set him apart from other people, to make him feared even without considering his lightning draw and unerring marksmanship.

A thought entered Derek's mind then that was new to him—something else marked Lashner as a man to be feared. He wasn't afraid to die. It was that simple. If a man were afraid to die he moved with kind of desperation. He might be fast, but it was not the same kind of speed possessed by another man who was cool and unafraid and calculating. He'd seen Lashner draw and fire, and knew that he was fast; yet some who had died before his gun might have been just as practiced as he, but had fallen before a cold nerve because they trembled inside.

A gray-clad stranger came hurrying up toward him, his eyes and the creases on his forehead showing worry and fear but his jaw grimly set with determination. 'I'm Travers,' he said. 'There's others on their way. Here come two now.'

It seemed then that they were rushing in from every direction. There were five of them, then seven, then nine and at last Ridge and Grayson hurried across the street, shotguns swinging at their sides.

'Everybody we talked to is here,' Ridge said. 'What you want us to do?'

'I'm going into the store,' Derek said. 'Put two men with shotguns in back. The rest of you stand out in the street facing the window.' He glanced around at the grim faces, saw that none wanted to hold back, and started up the boardwalk. When he reached the store he stopped and watched them spread out fanwise in front of him. Then he turned and went inside.

Robert was nowhwere in sight, but Lashner and Hees were standing alert and watchful. The gunman stood with his arms folded, waiting just inside the door. Hees was behind the counter, his apron thrown to one side and his right hand below Derek's line of vision.

Derek moved over beside the stove. 'Where's Robert Otis?' he demanded.

'Where you won't never find him!' Hees gritted savagely.

'If I don't, what do you think those men outside will do?'

Lashner's mask broke into a sneer. 'The brave Englishman brought his army with him against two men,' he taunted. 'Is that why you wouldn't fight Griff and Cervantes? 'Cause you didn't have an army?'

'Lashner,' Derek said softly, 'maybe you're a good teacher and maybe you're not. But if you're trying to earn that hundred dollars I promised you, it'll have to be another time. Right now you just come outside with me.'

Lashner looked out at the men on the boardwalk and said, 'Hees, you'll pay for causin' me to go out there. Only a damned fool'd try to take a man's kid. When I come back in here you'll pay.' He followed Derek through the door, fastened his eyes on the plump Grayson who stood in front of the others, and said, 'If anybody pulls a trigger I can kill three of you, maybe more, before I

161

hit the ground. And if anybody out there's got the guts, let him step up here and face me with a six-gun.'

Grayson spoke up grimly. 'Six-guns is your game, not ours. Ours is shotguns. But we ain't here to talk and play games. I'll count five and if you ain't headed for your horse by then I'll shoot both barrels right into your guts. Anybody else can shoot that wants to. One. Two. Three. Four—'

Lashner's face turned hard in the knowledge that there was no use trying to bluff it out, and no use trying to freeze them with his nerve. The man was counting too fast, was too anxious to pull the trigger.

He spun to his right and started moving toward his horse. He threw the reins over the stallion's neck and pulled himself up, his face swollen with anger. 'Now let me tell you somethin'—ever'one of you,' he shouted. ''Fore I get through there won't be no town here. It'll be leveled right down to the ground! And there won't be nobody here neither. Them that's able to run'll be lucky!'

Grayson's face swelled and turned even redder. 'An' I'll tell you somethin'!' he shouted back. 'You ever set foot in this town again and you're fair game. It don't matter where you're standin' or walkin' or which way you're lookin'—you're fair game for shotguns!'

Lashner looked down at Derek. 'The town

162

don't really matter none,' he said. 'You're the one that matters. There ain't enough shotguns in this state to keep me from gettin' you.' He whirled the stallion and savagely raked its flanks with sharp spurs. It moved off in a surging run, but he was barely out of shotgun range when his six-gun began to blast over his shoulder into the crowd. Travers groaned as a ball plowed into his shoulder and another man sat down heavily, nursing a wounded calf. Then two rifles began to fire steadily, and Lashner was forced to duck low over his saddle as he swung into the brush.

Travers sat down beside the shotgun that had dropped from his stiffened fingers. 'It'll teach us a lesson,' he groaned.

Grayson nodded in emphatic agreement. 'There's some men that's got to be killed, there ain't no other way. And the time to kill 'em is when you got the drop on 'em.'

Derek strode back into the store. Robert was still nowhere in sight, but Hees was standing at the end of the counter, his fingers gripping the butt of a six-gun strapped to his waist. His mouth was turned down at the corners, but he didn't seem to be afraid. 'The rest of it's up to you,' he said. 'I got the kid here behind the counter. You can save his life or lose it—it's up to you.'

Derek spread his feet in the way Lashner had taught him. 'It's not up to me,' he said. 'It's up to you. You're wearing a six-gun. You

163

can drop it to the floor and come out, or you can draw.'

'I'll make you a proposition,' Hees said. 'I'll ride out of this town and I'll never come back. The three of us'll leave here, you and me and the kid. When we get down the road a piece, you and the kid can come back.'

'The boy's not going any place,' Derek said.

'You better get somethin' straight,' Hees said. 'You ain't foolin' with no greenhorn. I've pulled this gun a few times an' I'm still here.'

'You'll have to pull it again if you don't come out.'

'I cain't come out,' he said hoarsely. 'You know that. You know what they'd do to me out there.'

'I'll talk to them,' Derek said. 'Put down your gun, and I'll talk to them.'

'I cain't put it down!' he roared. His tone lowered at once. 'If I get killed, you know what'll happen to you,' he warned. 'Lashner'll kill you. And if somethin' happens that he don't, Griff and Cervantes will get your cattle anyways. I'm the only one can stop 'em.'

Derek said softly, 'I might have figured that Griff and Cervantes worked for you, but I didn't.'

'They do,' Hees said triumphantly, 'and I'm the only one can stop 'em.'

'We'll talk about it after you've taken your gun off.'

'It ain't comin' off,' Hees warned. 'An' the only reason I'm arguin' ain't because of you, it's them others out there.'

'We've talked enough,' Derek said. 'You'li have to decide now. Drop it or draw it.'

In answer Hees savagely moved behind the counter, ducking and at the same time whipping his gun up. Only the top half of his head still remained above the counter when the leaden ball caught him in the middle of the forehead.

Derek cocked his six-gun and raced around after him, but the shooting was over and done with. Robert Otis huddled beside the dead Hees, his hands and feet tied and a gag crammed into his mouth. His eyes were wide with terror. Derek stepped over Hees and began to untie the boy, aware that the men from outside were flooding into the store now. They suddenly parted and made way for Sara Otis, who was screaming hysterically as she plowed between them.

As she staggered over Hees, Robert tried to rise. His cramped limbs responded slowly, but somehow he managed to get his arms up and around her neck and she lifted him. Tears were flowing freely down her cheeks and she was moaning, 'Thank God. Thank God. Thank God.'

Derek moved away from them and went

165

back around the counter to stand near the stove, his mind filled with strange thoughts. Grayson had said a few minutes ago that some people needed killing. There wasn't any other way. And the time to do it was when you had the drop on them. A few months ago he'd have rebelled at the idea, even though he'd killed other men in time of war. But just now he'd killed a man in personal combat, and while death still seemed ugly to him, he couldn't bring himself to feel any remorse.

'Hees's got a nephew over in Stantone,' someone remarked behind him. 'Likely he'll git the store, if anybody cares. For two cents I'd set a match to it.'

Grayson came up behind him and said, 'Mr. Langston, we got to thank you. There's no tellin' what we might've done if you hadn't come in here and got us together. And we know that just sayin' thanks ain't enough.'

'It took all of us,' Derek said. 'You know that.'

Grayson nodded. 'That's what I'm gittin' at. Sometimes it takes a lot of people to git somethin' done. An' Ben Ridge has been tellin' us what you're up against. Now, all of us put together don't have enough money to make up fer what Delphine Judson and us did to the bank, but there is one thing we can do. We can help you round up a herd o' cattle. There ain't none of us cowboys, mind you, and we cain't go on no drive, but some of us been talkin' and we figger, time we git through tellin' our friends, there'll be maybe forty men out to your ranch tomorrer. That way you'll git started in time, anyways.' He paused and seemed to have some trouble finding the right words. 'An' we all hope you'll come back after the drive and build up your ranch. You're the kind of neighbor we want.'

Derek looked at him almost unable to speak. It was a slim chance but better than none. And it was being given by the same people who'd been willing to stand by and watch Otis beat him into senselessness only a few weeks past.

'Then I'll expect you in the morning,' he said. And because he didn't trust himself to speak further, he started for his horse.

CHAPTER FIFTEEN

Their horses were exhausted and it was well past dark when Derek and Ridge rode into the clearing in front of the ranch house. The moon was waning but it was still bright enough to light up the countryside. Ridge saw Lashner behind every tree, but Derek refused to worry about him. 'He won't shoot from ambush,' he insisted. 'He'll want everyone to see me face him and lose.'

167

'Maybe,' Ridge growled. He spat. 'But a man that'll kidnap a kid ain't too low for nothin'!'

As he spoke a lamp was lighted within the ranch house walls and at the same time Ridge spotted the moonlit silhouettes of a strange horse and mule in the corral.

Derek loosened the six-gun in his holster and dismounted. 'Wait here a minute,' he said.

He advanced cautiously, but it was the big form of Billy Cedar that rose and smiled at him over the low walls. 'Been keepin' Sam company,' he said gravely. 'I've come to stay if you can use me.'

Derek grasped his hand, then turned and waved at Ridge.

'I seen who it was,' Ridge called. 'I'll take care of the horses.'

Sam Otis looked up eagerly. 'Is Sary all right? And Robert?'

Derek nodded. 'Everything's fine, Sam. How are you?'

'Doin' fine—'specially since Billy come.'

Derek sat down next to the fireplace and poured himself a steaming cup of coffee. 'You know I want you to stay, Billy. But you must know that I'm not good for much pay these days.'

Cedar came over and hunkered down beside him. 'Yeah, I know. I tried to reason with Delphine when I found out what

168

happened. I been arguin' with her for two days.' He relaxed against the wall and his left wrist automatically settled into his right hand. 'I even tried to scare her some, pointin' out that it's me keeps them cowhands in line over there, not her. But I reckon that ain't really true, and she knows it. Anyway, I ain't never seen her so unreasonable; she set out to break you and she's bound to do it. Told me if I come over here she'd treat me the same as you.'

'We'll give her a run for her money,' Derek said softly. 'We'll be moving a herd out of here by the middle of the week.'

'Sam says you've got twenty-eight head so far.'

Derek took a deep breath. 'About forty men are coming out tomorrow to help us. Farmers and townsmen.'

Cedar whistled through his teeth. 'Why?'

'They think I gave them a hand today.'

Sam Otis raised up on one elbow, suddenly frightened. 'Was it somethin' to do with Sary? Is that why she come out here?'

Derek said gently, 'I might as well tell you—Casper Hees tried to kidnap Robert. Grayson and Ridge got everybody together and ran Lashner out of town and I killed Hees. Robert wasn't hurt.'

Otis' face was creased with worry and his breathing was heavy. 'Is he really all right?'

'He's really all right, Sam. And he's

coming here with your wife tomorrow. They're going to take care of you while the rest of us are rounding up the cattle.'

Otis sank back on the blankets, the frown still between his eyes.

'Well,' Cedar said. 'We've got a job on our hands. We'll hit trouble seven ways to Sunday.'

Derek smiled. 'Are you already sorry you came to the Tower?'

Cedar shook his head gravely. 'Nope. You can count on me.'

'And on me,' Ridge said, stepping over the doorway.

*　　*　　*

Derek and Cedar and Ridge were up before the first pink fingers touched the gray sky, and by dawn Ridge was already galloping north to tell Corenson that the Tower herd would be with him when he left for Kansas.

When the hoofbeats died away Cedar said quietly, 'I reckon you've got some kind of plan all figgered out?'

Derek's answer was flat and positive. 'We're going to move onto the Strip. The roundup will be easier there, and I'll be ten miles closer to where I'm going before I even start.'

'All right,' Cedar said gravely. 'I know that Strip like the inside of my hand. I know a place where we can hold 'em with nothin' but a short brush fence—and figgerin' we run their legs off that first day to get 'em wore down some, we can go about nineteen miles and there's another good place to hold 'em that first night. Steep hills on one side and a big dry creek on t'other. After that we'll all be broke in a little and we'll strike out like a cat shot in the behind with a hot cracklin'.'

Derek grinned. 'That sounds fast enough.' He cocked his head, listening to the sounds of approaching wagons, and felt his load lightening with each passing second. 'They had to leave at midnight to get here this soon,' he marveled.

'There's something we need to talk about before they get here,' Cedar said. 'Delphine'll know about us goin' to the Strip 'fore we even get there.'

'I'm banking on what's happened in the past,' Derek answered. 'She destroyed my supplies but no one took a shot at me. And when she got all the money I had in the bank, that was done without shooting, too. I don't think she wants to kill anybody.'

'You might be right,' Cedar agreed. 'I wouldn't depend on it too much, but you got a point. You thought any about Griff and Cervantes and Lashner?'

'I've thought about them. And I've got to go ahead as though they didn't exist. They might be caught by surprise without enough

171

time to get a crew together. If not, then I'll fight them when the time comes.'

By then the first wagons were rolling up. The townspeople were going to treat the whole thing like a picnic, Derek decided; well-wrapped children were bedded down in some of the buckboards, and other wagons were stacked high with enough pots and pans to feed an army.

'There'll be a little grumblin',' Cedar grinned, 'when they find out they've got to keep goin'. But they'll get over it quick enough. I'll go give 'em the good news, and we'll get started.'

*   *   *

They left Sam Otis propped against a wall like a satisfied rooster, ready to direct any latecomers to the Strip. Sara, a soft rose suffusing her cheeks, looked almost pretty as she waved good-by. Robert was in the Grayson wagon, and Derek had the feeling that Sara and Sam were going to enjoy their time alone.

They set up camp on the bank of the river that ran through the Strip, and suddenly everything was working smoothly. Thirty-seven men had come in from town, most of them more eager than experienced, though, as Grayson said jocularly, 'There's some of us here worked the ranges before the war. Give us a chance to lose twenty pounds and I bet we're as good as we ever were!' But watching their wives join together and begin to set out the food, Derek had a notion they weren't going to lose twenty pounds on this roundup.

Just before the last of the plates had been wiped clean, the four cowhands Saltner had promised rode up and after Cedar talked to them he said to Derek, 'I'd rather have ten like them than the whole passel, but I reckon we can make do with what we got.' A breeze was coming up and he raised his collar, then cupped both hands over his mouth. 'Ever'body over here!' he shouted. 'Come right up here close so we can make talk.'

There was a great clattering of plates and cups as the men got up from their places at the campfire and strolled toward them. There didn't seem to be any hurry in any of them, and even less in Cedar. But Derek had the feeling that Cedar would know how to get the job done quickly, once the roundup was officially under way.

And there was a kind of anticipation in the air, a sense of excitement which hinted that the others were holding back in order to demonstrate an underlying confidence.

The day was bright with colors that gleamed in the March sunshine. The steady clacking of women's tongues was pierced from time to time by the shrill cries of running, whooping children, and Derek noticed that Robert Otis, none the worse for his ordeal, was lordly ordering his playmates around. And they were obeying without question. He was a hero today, a newly-awakened prince to the other children, and a little in awe of himself.

Derek grinned. The men were a little in awe of themselves, too, and they deserved every bit of praise anyone could think of. But they were a motley-looking lot. As they shuffled together he took special note, and saw that some were costumed in outfits as bright as a newly minted penny, and some had chosen their raggedest clothes for this occasion.

As he studied them closer his face sobered. A few wore leggings, but most didn't even have brush jackets, and over half were wearing high-topped shoes in place of boots. Several were not wearing guns and would be helpless before the onslaught of a crazed longhorn. Still, there were others to look after them. A full third were wearing their service revolvers, and he couldn't help remembering what Cedar had said just before Delphine had destroyed his own firearms—*Even the Yankees let us keep our guns!*

But guns weren't all they'd kept. It took a certain amount of spirit, too, to keep the military insignia of a defeated army pinned to the crowns of their wide-brimmed hats; and it was well to remember that even if they weren't top cowhands, they'd worked together before. But their faces were stamped with attitudes as different as night and day. Some seemed ready to take wild and unnecessary chances at the first pretext, and some appeared so cautious he doubted if they'd get far away from the fire.

Cedar squatted down before them and drew a diagram in the dirt with his index finger. 'This here's them banks way over there behind us,' he said. 'Bein' as they run from eight to fifteen feet high and they're straight up and down, we'll figger they can hold anything we put in there.' The line he drew showed the banks to be roughly U shaped, widening at the bottom of the U. 'We'll use brush to close this opening,' he said. 'We'll pile it up to build a funnel like this—and we'll make some kind of a gate that we can throw in to close the opening. While the rest of us are out gathering the cattle I'll want some to stay here and build a brush fence. Wherever there's a handy tree standin', use it for a post. Just do the best you can as fast as you can.' He stood up. 'Who'll stay behind and build the fence? The kids can help, if they want.'

Several appeared to want to stay, but no one seemed to want to admit it. 'The rest of us can work our heads off,' Derek said, 'and it's no good if that fence isn't up.'

One of the older men instantly spoke up. 'Well, puttin' it like that, I reckon there's

175

plenty of us got axes and machetes in our wagons. And I've built more kinds of fences than any man in the state of Texas.'

After several of the others agreed to join him, Cedar pushed back his hat and scratched his head. 'Then I got some things to tell the rest of you,' he said. 'Some know it and some don't. Them that do will just have to listen anyway.' He caught his hat as the breeze almost lifted it off his head, and said, 'There'll be room in that corral for maybe six hundred or a little more. The ones that seem like they're goin' to cause the most trouble, we'll cut out and turn loose. We'll cut out the cripples that cain't keep up on a drive and we'll cut out the skinny ones that ain't got enough fat to tide 'em over. We'll cut out cows about to drop calves, and mind this—we'll cut out any that're colored up white and such—they might spook the whole bunch on a moonlit night. What's left, we'll drive out of here. Anybody got any questions now?'

A bearded farmer spoke up. 'Yeah. How we goin' to do this? Will we work in little bunches, or all together?'

'We'll start out all together,' Cedar said. 'We ain't goin' far from camp 'fore we fan out. Then, makin' sure all the women and kids are clear, we'll ride through the brush and try to start 'em driftin' this way. Not spookin' em any more'n we have to. The

176

wildest ones—the ones that cut back through us—we'll let go. We'll see how many we get that way. If it don't work out we'll do somethin' else. Let's get started now.' He called back over his shoulder, 'We're dependin' on havin' that fence just as soon as we can get it!'

Derek rode off beside Cedar, and a half hour later the whole outfit fanned out and started the drive for camp. The men were a little nervous but yelling from sheer pleasure sometimes because they were a group of people doing something together—and perhaps because if any one of them failed to do his job properly it was nothing to be ashamed of. None could make any mistake that would be held against him as long as he kept life and limb intact.

The longhorns did not graze in large herds; and when they were surprised they bolted away with the speed of deer, and as often as not kept going until they were beyond both reaches of the drive. Horns flashed like swords and pounded tree limbs like clubs. The whooping and hollering grew louder in spite of Cedar's instructions; and some of the men tore through the thickets like an avalanche, while others tightly hugged the clearings. More than once the roundup seemed doomed to complete failure; but because the cattle here were far more docile than those on the upper, drier ranges, a few head began to drift in the right direction in spite of the confusion.

'For cripe's sake, shut up and let 'em drift!' Cedar shouted.

Some of the exuberance faded away and the men began to follow the animals more quietly. The system worked, and discounting prickly-pear thorns, bruises from hard limbs, and a few raw scratches from mesquite and huisache, the whole crew reached camp without casualties and were able to pen a full forty head.

Of the lot, ranging in color from solid red to red-and-white speckled to solid white, with duns and brindles and one black thrown in for good measure—and ranging in age from three to ten years or more—only six wore the Tower brand.

Cedar rode up to Derek, who sat his horse alongside the edges of the barely started brush fence. 'We'll have to leave three or four men behind now,' he observed, 'and they'll have to watch like hawks to keep them longhorns from stampedin' out of here and runnin' over ever'body. The rest of us had best get started. We'll have to go fu'ther this time, an' we'll have to hurry to make it back by sundown.'

'Can you tell yet how soon we'll have a herd?' Derek asked.

'Nope,' Cedar said flatly. 'Tomorrer won't be like today. Tomorrer they'll realize they're

178

workin'. But we'll get another forty head or so 'fore this day's over.' He grinned. 'An' tonight they'll all be struttin' like peacocks.'

★   ★   ★

The activity around camp at sundown bore out his words. After tallow-fried beef and beans were wolfed down, pots and tin plates had to be scoured by the women, and teams looked after by the men; but it was all accomplished with a feverishness that bespoke a soon-to-be-received reward for a day's work well done.

The chores were finished while the sky to the west still showed traces of the orange-purple of sunset. The brisk breeze they'd felt all day had died to a wisp of movement that barely fanned the central campfire and gently riffled small waves in the slow-moving river. Some of the older children heaped wood onto the fire and the plump Grayson, who only yesterday had held a shotgun in his hands and roared defiance at Lashner, began softly to strum his guitar.

The others moved up silently and gathered around him as his voice lifted in song.

The years creep slowly by, Lorena,
The snow is on the grass again.

A few husky male voices joined in almost at
179

once, and then, more slowly, the higher notes of the women and children were added, until the words rang out sweet and strong and plaintive—

The sun's low down the sky, Lorena,
The frost gleams where the flow'rs have
been.

Derek hunkered down with his back to a wagon wheel, nodding a greeting as Billy Cedar moved over beside him. Cedar squirmed, hating to interrupt but still wanting to talk. It was impossible for Derek not to incline his head toward him, but he couldn't help thinking that Cedar was the only man in the state of Texas he'd have forgiven for interrupting his reverie.

'They'll not be singin' so much tomorrer night,' Cedar observed. 'Their muscles'll be screamin' and they'll be thinkin' second thoughts and some of 'em'll be lookin' around for excuses to be goin' back to town. But they'll stick—all of 'em. Each one'll be afraid to say anythin' for fear of what all the others'd think.'

For a moment Derek thought Cedar might be feeling his way toward a complaint against the lot of them, but he knew at once that he was wrong. The man had simply wanted to talk and had not known how to begin.

He smiled. 'Someone listening might say

180

you didn't have a very high opinion of your fellow countrymen.'

Cedar said instantly, 'No, I didn't mean it like that. I like 'em all and I think I understand 'em all. Most of 'em, anyway. I know that some'll quit when the goin' gets tough, and I know some are scared to move for fear somethin'll happen to 'em. But I can understand all that 'cause I've quit a time or two myself. And God knows, I've been scared.'

Derek said slowly, 'Maybe all of us do what we think we have to do in order to be safe. Maybe that's what we're doing even when we take chances. But what about the ones who won't care? The ones like Lashner? Even when we ran him out of town he wasn't frightened.'

Cedar blinked his eyes as a curl of smoke drifted into his face. 'I've seen some like that,' he admitted. 'Not many. Near as I can make out, they ain't afraid to die and that's all there is to it.'

Derek nodded in agreement. They were singing 'Ever of Thee I'm Fondly Dreaming,' and he wanted to listen, but Cedar was determined to talk.

'Men like Lashner are just a handful,' he said. 'But you take somebody like Gort—most of us might be like him if it came right down to it. Gort ain't no more scared of dyin' or gettin' hurt than the rest of us, but

181

durin' the war—he's young, mind you—him and another soldier was supposed to hold a place. Gort would've stuck, too, but the other feller ran, and the first thing Gort knew, he was runnin' too. It wasn't like him at all, but he did it. Now ever'body knows about it, an' he's still tryin' to make up for it. The rest of us, we can forget about the war, but Gort, he's got to prove over and over again—ever' single day—that he ain't scared. Which just helps prove that all of us are scared of one thing, even Lashner.'

Derek asked curiously, 'What?'

'What the other feller thinks. Half of what Lashner does is 'cause he wants other people to be afraid of him, and think he's really somethin'. And half of what all of us do or don't do is for the same reason, just like I said before. It takes lots more guts to stand up to people who think different from you than it does to fight 'em with your fists.'

'Do you think Delphine Judson gives a damn what anybody else thinks?'

The question caught Cedar by surprise. 'Well—it's hard for me to figger Delphine bein' different from anybody else. So I guess she must care what people think. But maybe not. A lot of people don't give a damn about anything while they're mad, an' she's had a mad on for a long time.' His right hand unconsciously slid over to grasp his left wrist. 'But I've got to tell you this much. I don't

182

like some of the things she does and I'm here right now doin' somethin' she don't want me to do, but I still feel like she's my daughter. An' I worry about her. Sometimes I get worried sick. Somebody like that—it's like a man with brittle bones—you've got to figger on somethin' breakin' sooner or later. Some bad things happened to her and she took 'em to heart too much.'

Derek was aware suddenly that the music had stopped and Grayson was calling to him from the other side of the campfire. 'You sing something, Mr. Langston. Sing an English song!'

Cedar was relieved at the interruption. 'Go ahead,' he said. 'They'll like that.'

Derek smiled. 'I'll sing a Scottish one, if you like,' he called back. 'We used to sing it a lot when we were fighting the Russians.' He thought for a second, and then began—

Maxwellton's braes are bonny,
Where early fa's the dew—

Grayson's nimble fingers immediately went into action and the guitar took up the melody of the old familiar song.

An' 'twas there that Annie Laurie
Ga' me her promise true.

Derek's voice lifted high and the words

poured out. For a moment he could almost picture himself beside another campfire in the long ago past, when the cold was colder and the sky overhead darker, when this song brought up the vision of a woman's face to men far from home. A face you couldn't recognise but one you were sure you'd know when the time came. And now he sang it and the face in the dancing flames took form against his will.

Ga' me her promise true,
Which ne'er forgot will be,
And for bonny Annie Laurie
I'd lay me doon and dee.

The strains lingered and echoed back across the riffling waters of the river. 'That was about as purty as a tune can get,' Grayson said. 'Let's have another.'

'Yeah,' a farmer said, 'let's hear one we ain't never heard before.'

'By tomorrow night I'll think of one,' Derek promised.

'Well,' Grayson said, 'we don't like to crowd nobody, but tomorrer night's a long time.'

'Then I'll make up for it with two songs.'

'All right,' Grayson said abruptly. 'We won't forget. And the truth is, I'm plumb wore out and just beginnin' to have sense enough to realize it. Anybody else wants to

184

sing, they can borry my guitar.'

It was a common sentiment and the camp began to bustle with activity again as bedding was dragged out and spread on the ground, and kids were shushed and shooed up into the wagons to sleep. Derek answered at least a dozen friendly 'good nights' and squirmed back against the wagon wheel.

'I guess you know what I'm thinking about,' he said.

'Yeah.' Cedar stood up and brushed off the seat of his pants. 'I got the notion you were thinkin' about Delphine while you were singin', and you haven't got her out of your mind yet. You want to know what she's apt to do, and you think because I know her better than most, I can tell you. But I cain't.'

He made a rolling motion with his shoulders, stretched, and changed the subject completely. 'They'll all sleep like dead people tonight,' he observed. 'An' I'm bettin' you won't be singin' any song for 'em tomorrer night, 'cause the men'll all be bedded down before the women've got the pots washed.' He grinned. 'I see I'm givin' my countrymen hell again. An' I'll say good night on that.' The grin left his face. ''Cept for one thing. It was Gort I really come to talk about. But I guess you knew that. Good night.'

'Good night.' Derek waited in deep thought until Cedar had disappeared beyond the wagons. Then he picked up his bedroll

185

and carried it to a knoll that overlooked the river. He dropped the bedding, stared up at the diamond-sharp stars piercing the black velvet sky, and wondered briefly why he was here at all. This heritage he was fighting for—it wasn't the same as the one which had been handed down to him from generations past. It was true that something here had attracted him beyond his capacity to resist; he could never sell out now and be happy somewhere else. But why did he want it, really? Because of a sense of power that came with ownership?

No, it wasn't that at all. A man did like to own something, for his own convenience—but he was concerned, too, with making his mark on the land and leaving something behind him after he was gone—and with having somebody to love and care for while he was here. It was all tied in together, and the girl who kept crowding into his mind as a part of it was the one person in the world who could keep him from succeeding. He could fight Griff and Cervantes and Lashner with guns, but what could he do if Delphine blocked his way?

He opened the bedroll and sank down onto it, wondering why Cedar had wanted to talk about Gort. Was it because the man had once shown fear, and he thought Derek might do the same? Or was it because Gort had acted in haste, and was living a long time to regret it?

There were axioms for the uninitiated to learn about handling cattle. Before midmorning a man had crowded a longhorn against a cutbank and when the crazed animal could find no other avenue of escape he had whirled and charged savagely at horse and rider. Luckily the would-be cowboy raised his leg in time to dodge the slashing horns but the horse's belly was ripped until its guts spilled out onto the ground. The steer crashed its way to freedom, its bloody horn a symbol of power and independence. The man was left behind, shaken and lowered in stature, to shoot his horse and walk back to camp with the saddle flung over his shoulder.

Before noon, another of the farmer-cowboys roped a stubborn old bull who refused to budge from beneath several low-hanging limbs. But after the rope settled about his neck he made a desparate lunge for freedom and the horse, caught sideways and unprepared, was jerked flat on its side. The rider, flung free, was the longhorn's next target. But Derek planted a ball from his six-gun in the middle of a hairy forehead in bare time to save the man's life.

There were axioms, too, about riding hell-for-leather through the thick, thorny brush. A man who did it without the proper equipment was a damned fool. And one of the men who had an outfit and who should have known better ducked his head to protect his eyes and keep his face from being scratched. That man was lucky, too. A tree limb knocked him senseless, but his feet did not hang up in the stirrups; and to be clubbed senseless was better than riding blindly into a limb that was broken into a sharp spear.

One hand, working Mexican style with his rope not tied to his saddlehorn, and too inexpert or too careless, was rope-burned so badly that the flesh was gouged out, raw and deep, refusing for a time even to bleed heavily.

Another broke a small bone in his arm when he was flung from his saddle as his horse jumped a gully while he looked back over his shoulder. But some were learning, too. The majority were quieter when they had to be, noisier when it helped, more aware of what they were trying to do, and more anxious to get the job over and done with.

The tally that day was one hundred and fifty head.

Billy Cedar had been right about one thing: there was no singing that night. Clouds were gathering thicker overhead and the wind was blowing and muscles were bone tired and screaming. It was a night to bed down early. But there was a kind of satisfaction in the whole undertaking, not only to Derek but to all the others. It was a big job, a hard job, and it was getting done in spite of the odds.

On the third day Jackson and the three other men Derek had sent for arrived. Derek made the same deal with them that he'd made with the four who had arrived earlier. He could pay them for thirty days. If they worked longer they'd be taking a chance. He'd give them double if the drive were a success, and they'd get nothing if he failed. It was a good gamble. In thirty days they'd know a hell of a lot about what was going to happen.

'Saltner heard about your drive,' Jackson added. 'There's a chuck wagon and cook'll get here in the mornin'.'

In late afternoon Derek rode up to the brushy side of the corral and watched several of the men pulling a struggling white animal out the gate. Cedar got down off his horse beside him and said, 'When they get that spook out of there you'll have three hundred and seventy-eight left. It's a damn sight better'n I really figured, and maybe more'n we can handle. But we'll lose some along.' He shook his head. 'I been on some rough roundups with some green hands, but this is the damnedest thing I ever been mixed up in.' He looked up seriously. 'These people here been mighty good about ever'thin'. Now it's your turn to do somethin' for them.'

'Like what?'

'Soon's we get started out of here in the mornin', you send 'em home. Men, women, kids and all. Maybe you'll get off this Strip without nobody bein' hurt and maybe you won't. But I talked to one of Delphine's hands about an hour ago, and he said she ain't goin' to put up with it. He says you won't get twenty miles and that's for sure. Delphine's boilin' mad and the whole crew's spoilin' for a fight.'

CHAPTER SIXTEEN

A mist began to swirl in at midnight, and the morning dawned a cold wintry gray. Derek cast his rope about the dun's neck with fingers that were stiff and numb; his whole body was strained and tight, and not even a monumental effort could keep his teeth from chattering. The townspeople were already starting to break camp. He wanted to go to each wagon and thank them individually, but Cedar was anxious to start the herd moving, and the noise and confusion were indescribable. To the chorus of bellowing cattle was added the barking of two dogs brought by one of the cowhands, the shrill cries of the children, commands by their parents, and the clank and rattle of tinware being heaped into the wagons.

As he led the dun back into camp Grayson rode up and thrust a steaming cup of coffee at him, yelling, 'Three of us'll ride drag for you a piece. And you better get saddled. Cedar's champin' at the bit.'

Derek nodded. 'Thanks!' The boiling thick liquid lent a spurious warmth which lasted only a minute or two. He put the cup aside, cinched his saddle tight against a braced belly and mounted. The first wagons were already starting to swing south, hurried along by men who cast apprehensive glances at the heavy skies. He waved, and rode up to the corral as the brush barriers were swept aside.

The cattle poured out, forced to move north into the swirling mist. Derek fell in alongside them and lightly raked the dun with blunt spurs to keep even with the first surge. For the first few hundred yards it was like trying to control an avalanche. The longhorns mushroomed out, turned and began to mill. But gradually a semblance of order and direction was achieved. After a time Derek was able to swing in the saddle to observe the long line strung out behind him. In its own way, he thought, the spectacle was as terrible and beautiful as an army with banners marching into battle. Violence was here, and power, ready to be unleashed with explosive fury and barely held in check.

He whirled his horse and yelled, 'Ei-yaa!' at a brindle cow that seemed hell bent on

191

regaining her freedom. The longhorn turned belligerently back into place, her split hoofs showering Derek with bits of mud.

Cedar had said that ground which sounded hollow was a menace, and it seemed to Derek that they were moving across a tightly-stretched drum. But maybe it was only his imagination. The mist had turned into a drizzling rain, whipped by little gusts of wind into his ears and down his neck, and maybe that affected his hearing. He was soaked to the skin already, his muscles tense and sore from straining against the piercing cold.

The drizzle began to turn into a downpour. Grayson waved at his two fellow townsmen and galloped his horse up to Derek, leaving a thin sheet of spray in his wake. 'I reckon we'll have to light a shuck,' he called out. 'You just don't know what happens when it rains in this country. Another two, three hours and we cain't even cross a wagon-sized gully!'

Derek waved, cupped one hand and shouted, 'Thanks for your help!'

Grayson grinned. 'It was a pleasure! There ain't one man here didn't enjoy it!' He whirled his horse, joined the two other men, and all three rode away, waving.

The rain beat down now like balls of hail, and the wind whipped it in sheets so that ponchos offered scant protection. Every man in the crew was already soaked to the bone and rigid from the cold. The massed longhorns gave out a kind of odor-filled heat that could be felt on the right flank, but even that was quickly dissipated and swirled away.

Because of the rain there was no sense of distance gained, no chance to establish a marker, move up to it, and past it, and then see it in the distance behind you. The land underfoot looked the same as the land they had already passed, and it was sometimes hard to believe they were moving. As the morning dragged on the rain slackened, but it quickly began again. By midday even the lowing of the cattle had given way to a grim silence. The mud grew thicker with each plodding step, and the cowboys seemed to come out of their shells only when a shrill yell and waving arms became necessary to halt a longhorn's bolt for freedom.

About twenty had made it, Derek guessed. But in the unfathomable ways of cattle at least eight had come prancing out of the brush to join the herd.

He had not seen this part of the Strip before and now, through the heavy torrents of rain, he visualized it as a gigantic boot some twenty miles long, narrowing properly as it came toward the ankle. Once it might have been some enormous river bed, before the river itself narrowed and shrank, for it was easily three miles wide, and sunk from ten to twenty feet below the surface of the

193

surrounding country. To the right lay what had once been a cutbank, but was now smooth and rounded from the erosion of centuries; to the left rose a string of low, broken hills. And between the two, the winding, twisting river, powder dry, they said, at the end of the long, hot summer, a pleasant murmur of running water last night, and today a whirling, mad, unreasoning current, laced with mud and debris. It was the heart and soul of the forty square miles called the Strip, and its normal course was clearly marked for all to see by the thin belt of sycamores and live oaks which lined each bank.

An enormous sycamore whirled into view carrying on its branches a huddled wildcat, wet and cold and shivering. A dead deer followed it, and then two longhorns; the river was swelling by the moment, even though the sky was turning a lighter gray and the rain was slackening again.

Up ahead the herd began to turn right, climbing the muddy banks to higher ground. For a moment Derek thought Cedar had turned them for fear the torrent would engulf the entire Strip. Then he saw through the last swirling mists that they had been moving straight toward a massed group of riders who blocked the Strip at its narrowest point between cutbank and river. And the nagging nervous tension that had ridden with him all day became a hard knot in his belly.

He lightly touched the spurs to the dun's flank and splashed his way up ahead. Cedar was hunched in his saddle, his narrowed eyes watching the soaked cowboys yell and prod and pressure the herd up out of the Strip. Derek drew rein beside him and nodded toward the blocked passage. 'Delphine?'

'It's her.' Cedar shivered slightly as the last of the herd thudded up onto high ground. 'People are funny about fightin',' he said. 'You push straight into somebody, they'll fight ever' time. But you let 'em get set like she is, an' then go around, it throws 'em off balance. That's why I had them turn the herd.'

The knot in Derek's belly coiled and tightened. 'This is the time I've dreaded,' he said. 'I don't want to fight Delphine. But I won't give up my herd and lose everything because a woman's hardheaded and stubborn!'

A lone rider shot out from Delphine's crew and raced toward them, splashing a wide path as the horse slapped over the pools of water.

When he reached them and slid to a stop, Cedar said, 'Hello, Gort.'

The young cowpuncher grinned, taking off his hat and shaking some of the water from it. 'Hello, Billy. Miss Delphine said to tell you you still got time to come over with us where you belong.'

'Is that all she sent you for?'

Gort grinned wider. 'Nope. She wants to talk to the Englishman here.'

'You know my name!' Derek said tightly. 'What does she want?'

'I reckon she'll tell you when you get there.'

'You mean you don't really know!'

The grin left Gort's face. 'Nope. That ain't what I mean a-tall. And you might as well know now as later—she says she's got a claim to these cattle the same as you have. And you ain't leavin' here with them unless you pay her three dollars a head for the whole lot.'

'You know he doesn't have any money left,' Cedar said.

Gort nodded. 'I know it and she knows it too. I reckon that's why she's doin' it. She says she'll give you time to get the herd bedded down and pitch camp. Then you hightail it on over there. We'll still be there—camped on the high ground just above where we are now.' He whirled his horse, said, 'See you, Billy,' and started back, galloping hard.

Cedar shook water off his hat and said, 'Well, we can fly off seven ways at once, or we can take each thing as it comes. It's up to you.'

From long habit, Derek ran the ball of his thumb across his mustache. There was nothing he wanted to do more than see

196

Delphine and get it over with. But after years in the Service he'd grown used to waiting; sometimes it had to be done even while the enemy set up their guns in plain sight.

'We'll talk to Delphine after we're settled,' he said.

Cedar set up camp some three hundred yards to the south of the bedding ground, where the steady cold north wind blew across the herd. 'A sound can set 'em off,' he said, 'but the smells are more important. They might stand still for a thunderstorm, then smell a pot of meat cookin' and light out all at once like a banshee was after 'em.'

It was still cold but the rain had stopped and a few patches of blue sky showed through the clouds. The smell of frying beef, simmering beans and boiling coffee hung heavy in the air as Derek pulled up to the chuck wagon. The bearded, piratical-looking old cook grinned up at him and proffered the inevitable cup of coffee, thick and strong and bitter. Derek sipped it and swung his stiff aching body off the dun.

The food probably wouldn't be any better than the coffee, he thought, but at least this man had had presence of mind enough to carry dry wood along with him in the wagon, and had the foresight now to keep wet sticks close to the fire where they could steam dry.

He tied the dun to a bush a few yards from camp and moved over to the fire. Only Billy

197

Cedar and the men on night duty were missing. The rest jostled and joked as they turned and twisted before the flames, letting the warmth dry their clothes. Looking at them, his nostrils filled with the smells evaporating from them, Derek couldn't help wondering which, if any, he could depend on. With the exceptions of Jackson and Billy Cedar, there wasn't one man there he knew.

Cedar rode up and a sudden, uncomfortable silence fell. He spotted Derek and said gravely, 'We can go now if you want to get it off your mind before you eat.'

Jackson thrust forward toward Derek. 'You know I ain't no fighter—I told you that when I hired on. But I got to say this—if it's a fight we've got to have, then we'd do better hittin' 'em tonight. And I ain't sure that ain't what they'll do to us if you go over there and don't get things settled.'

'I'll do my own worrying,' Derek said sharply.

'And that goes for me, too,' Jackson said stubbornly. 'It's your herd but if we get in a fight a bullet'll treat me the same way it will you.'

'But you'd still be willing to fight for my herd?'

'We all got a share in it,' Jackson said. 'You paid us for thirty days. We're gamblin' on the rest.'

Derek looked at Cedar. 'Let's go, Billy.

Let's go settle this.'

★   ★   ★

Delphine was camped on a promontory extending almost to the river. A huge gray boulder nearby reared up against the dimming skyline and a guard, rifle across his knees, sat on top of it. Other, lesser boulders nestled up close and it was south of this line that Delphine had chosen to camp. Perhaps a dozen men ringed the large, roaring fire, while another in the background rattled plates in a wash pan. But neither sounds nor smells were apt to reach the longhorns with the promontory jutting this far to the west.

Delphine was seated on a small rock between the fire and the guarding boulders. She made no effort to get up as Derek and Cedar rode up to her and dismounted. A wary silence hung over the camp and Delphine's hostility could almost be smelled.

'You know why I'm here,' Derek said finally.

Delphine looked up at him and her eyes shone sharp and angry beneath the black brim of her hat. 'You're here because I sent for you!'

'I won't argue the point,' Derek said. 'I'm here because I want to prevent a fight if I can.'

Delphine wet her lip. 'You can. Give me

three dollars a head and you'll have no fight.'

'You know I can't do that. You know that the only thing left is for me to fight. And you know that if we do fight there'll be men killed on both sides.'

She nodded shortly. 'My men are hired to fight when they have to.'

'But they don't have to now.'

'Then they're hired to fight when I say to!'

Cedar said softly, 'Delphine—'

'You're not in this,' she snapped. 'This is between me and Derek Langston.'

'Then I'd better point out somethin' to you,' Cedar said. 'You think it's between you and him, and that you'll win. That's what Hees thought, too. And now he's buried.'

Delphine stood up and brushed off a stray wisp of ash from her blue denims. 'It won't be the same,' she said. 'If he wins and I live, we'll fight again. If he wins and I'm dead he'll never hear the end of it. He'll always be the Englishman who fought a woman and killed her.'

'You're overlooking something,' Derek said. 'You're overlooking the fact that I'm reaching a point where I don't give a damn one way or the other. I've been pushed and squeezed and held back by you and Hees and others like you, until I'm not even sure I want to win. I just want to see how many I can pull down with me when the time comes.'

'Then there's nothing left to do but see if

you mean it.'

Cedar swung up first and Derek agreed that it was a futile argument. He mounted the dun and whirled it, and they moved off in the darkness back toward their own camp.

They neared the herd and began a wide circle and Cedar said, 'I heard what you said for Delphine's benefit. Now you might as well say what you really mean to do.'

'What can I do?' Derek demanded.

'Since you ain't got money,' Cedar said, 'there's only two things. You can give up or fight. And I might as well tell you I cain't fight Delphine. I know she's wrong but I cain't bring myself to do it.'

'Then why the hell didn't you stay in her camp while you were there?'

'Because maybe somethin' can still be done about it. If I didn't think there was a chance I never would have started helpin' you in the first place.'

'You have something in mind?'

'Only one thing. I can go back and see her again—alone. And this time maybe I can make a deal with her.'

'Like what?'

'Like sayin' that if she lets you through with this herd, she can have the Strip. Now and forever.'

It was hard to make out Cedar's face in the darkness, but Derek felt himself turning hot all over with murderous rage. 'This is what

201

you've had in mind since the day you came to help me, isn't it?'

'Yes,' Cedar said. 'I reckon it is.'

'Did she send you to me in the first place?'

'Nope. I come on my own. The way I saw it, if you didn't get a herd through you'd lose everything, so maybe you'd be willing to make a settlement. But I knew the two of you couldn't ever work things out unless I helped. I did the only thing I could think of.'

Derek lapsed into silence, but the rage still burned in him.

'There's somethin' else to figger,' Cedar said. 'If there's a fight, you won't have no herd. The minute the shootin' starts they'll scatter to hell and you'll be right back where you started. You'd be better off losin' the Strip and losin' face, and savin' what you can.'

They reached camp, hobbled their horses and turned them loose, then moved up to the fire. The men were tense and they half-rose as Derek came close.

'What's it to be?' Jackson demanded. 'Fight or give up? Because we already talked it over and if it's a fight we want it to be tonight, while we've got some edge.'

Over and over the thought had been working in Derek's mind. If they had a fight he was through, no matter whether he won or lost. He wouldn't have the herd and he wouldn't have Cedar to help him and if some of the crew got killed or hurt he wouldn't have them either. And he'd be thinking for the rest of his life that if he hadn't fought, they'd still be alive. And worse—suppose Delphine Judson got killed? He must be out of his mind even to be concerned, but he couldn't stop thinking about it. He could look into the campfire now and see her face there. He'd done it before and sometimes the hard lines went away and the face was soft and relaxed and smiling.

He hardened his jaw. 'There's nothing left but to give up something,' he said. 'If I give up the herd I'm ruined. If I give up the Strip, my ranch will be harder to operate for the rest of my life.' He turned to Cedar. 'You go back to Delphine in the morning. Before daylight. Maybe when we're close to a fight, she won't be so hardheaded. You tell her that after I get the herd to market, and get paid for them, I'll give her three dollars a head. For the whole lot. That way she'll save face and make a lot more profit than she's entitled to—and I'll save the ranch, including the Strip.'

Jackson snorted. 'Hell, man, you cain't start payin' off people like this! Don't you know what we're goin' to run into on the trail?'

A cowboy named Burton, with a round, babyish face and round eyes, chipped in. 'Hell, we'll be crossin' Injun territory. The Injuns'll ride down and say, "Give us thirty head and we won't start no stampede." You give it to them and there'll be more Injuns ten miles down the trail and more after that. If you got any cattle left after you get across their territory, there'll be jayhawkers to take 'em. You cain't make no payoff. Not even one.'

'This one is different,' Derek insisted. 'I'm not losing any of the cattle. It's money I'm losing. Money that belongs to me. I can do with it as I see fit.'

Burton shook his head. 'You're overlookin' what Jackson said before, mister. You paid us for thirty days. We're gamblin' on the rest. But it ain't no gamble if you're goin' to start makin' payoffs. Hell, I ain't even about fixin' to go if you're goin' to pay out one head of stock or one dollar!'

'You don't have to go,' Derek said. 'You can ride away tonight if you want to! Don't forget, Billy,' he added, 'before daylight.'

He picked up his bedroll from the wagon and trudged through the mud away from the campfire to a spot of ground that was drier than the rest. He heard a heated conversation going on behind him. *Let them argue. Let them quit if they wanted to!* The one thing that might hold them was the fact that jobs were scarce. If that didn't do it he doubted if anything would.

He slammed the bedroll savagely down to the ground. There was another good reason for him not to hang around the campfire. When a man reached the point where he could handle a gun as he could, there was a big temptation to use it sometimes when there was really no need for it. He'd felt a violence growing in him daily since the moment he'd taken the Webley out of his saddlebag and put it in his belt. He'd felt it rise to the point where he'd forced Hees into a fight and then killed him. Now because it was a woman who blocked his way and because that woman was Delphine Judson, he was forcing himself to do nothing when the violence swelled in him and threatened to explode. But he couldn't hold it much longer; not for anybody. A few more words around the campfire and his gun might come out.

He shucked off his boots and gun belt and crawled into the bedroll, keeping the Remington in his hand. Why was it he wanted to kill somebody? he wondered; that wasn't the kind of man he'd been before he'd come here. But that day when he'd put the Webley in his belt he'd stepped into a river as wild and swirling as the one down below him now. And once you set foot in it there was no turning back. You had to go wherever it took you and fight to keep afloat.

Well, he'd fought. He'd ridden the river around every bend and turn. And the violence in him still said fight, and some of his reason joined with it. He'd be bound to

205

lose his herd, but at least he'd keep his self-respect. That was what he would do in the morning, then, if Cedar failed. If some of his cowboys ran out, the ones who stuck would have to fight alongside him. If they all ran out, he'd have to fight alone. He'd make sure Delphine wasn't harmed, but he'd fight her crew as long as there was a breath in him.

The fury burned in his mind for a time, and then he fell into an exhausted and fitful sleep.

CHAPTER SEVENTEEN

In his sleep Derek heard the belligerent bellowing of driven cattle, the cries of working cowhands, could feel the muffled thuds of split hoofs sloshing in soft mud.

And then he was awake and the dream was reality. The herd had already been driven down from the high ground and across the narrow Strip, was already plunging into the raging, still rising river. For a startled instant he could not believe his eyes. Then he saw below him the abandoned camp, the empty wagon, the dead fire.

It struck him that not one member of his crew had remained with him, else he'd have heard warning shots. They must have waited until Cedar had started for Delphine's camp, and then quietly drifted away. But if Delphine were taking his herd, why hadn't Cedar at least warned him?

He saw then that it was not Delphine. Through the gray of the early dawn he spied one familiar form and then another—Griff and Cervantes fulfilling the promise they had made him weeks ago.

He begrudged the feverish seconds it took to pull on his boots and fasten his gun belt; the minutes it took to find his bridle and look around for the dun. Impatience burned in him until the cold air was no longer cold, and he had a notion that no person he had ever known except Rig Lashner could understand the way he felt this minute. He was barely conscious of the thumb that dug under his belt, of the spreading fingers that pointed toward his cattle. It was only a momentary thing, and the hand swung free as he started for the steep edge of the cutbank.

The horse was down on the Strip, perhaps four hundred yards from camp, contentedly munching the soaked grass. After Derek spotted him it took every bit of patience he possessed to keep from racing up to him. But he steeled himself, maintained his steady trot and finally slowed to a walk as the dun saw him and threw back his head. He approached the animal gently, spoke to him in a soft voice and slipped the bridle into place.

When the hobbles were removed he slid up

onto the bare back and looked left toward the herd. They had been driven into the river at the only possible crossing—a narrow chiseled area where both banks sloped gently down to the water. Even then many of the crazed animals were being swept downriver and lost in the swirling currents. But most were making it, were struggling through and out on the other side.

Something on the cutbank above and to his right caught his eye and he prodded the dun with bare boot heels. The horse surged forward and he glimpsed a dark-clad figure looking down at him, saw the man sliding his rifle from his saddle scabbard. Cervantes had come back for him.

Derek reined in against the bank. A gully cut into the higher land mass only a few feet in front of him. He urged the dun into it.

The gully was filled with pools of shallow water and floored with a scattering of rounded pebbles. The high ground was above the top of his head here, but further on the gully grew narrower and shallower. His temple would be in Cervantes' rifle sights in another twenty yards. He slid off the dun and let the animal keep going.

The mud and gravel clawed at him, raked his body. The earth seemed to wrap around him like a muddy blanket. He slammed to a dizzying stop, rolled over, and struggled to his knees. He tried to wring the mud off his gun hand, then inched forward and sloshed his palm in a pool of water.

The dun's hoofs still clattered wildly in front of him, but they were slowing now. He heard Cervantes up on the high ground riding swiftly to cut him off. He wiped his wet hand on a dry spot on his trousers and drew the Remington.

At a bend in the gully Cervantes plowed to a stop and looked toward the running horse. But the steely click of the six-gun's hammer reached his ears and he whirled, his rifle jamming against his shoulder. The desperate search for a target took only a fraction of a second, but the interval was too long. The curled hammer fell and the rifle dropped from Cervantes' fingers as he clawed at his chest. For a moment he tried to hang onto the saddlehorn, but the strength in his body diminished and turned to ashes. He slid free and slumped to the ground.

Derek clattered up the slick, wet stones of the gully, his gun still held ready. He reached the dead Cervantes and stood over him. The rage burning in him said that he'd see Griff like that too before this day was over. And as many more as he could take with him.

Cervantes' black stallion shied away from him, but he spoke softly, gently, and at last caught the animal's reins. The horse reared as he mounted, then lunged forward. But the hard Spanish bit turned him easily. He started at a dead run for the river, his churning hoofs throwing up fist-size chunks of slick mud as they plunged down the steep cutbank.

As they hit the Strip the horse slid, caught stride and raced on. Derek felt behind the saddle for Cervantes' poncho and wrapped the six-gun in it.

The cattle were across now, all that would ever make it. Upriver, where a wedge-shaped slice of high ground split the raging torrent, a dozen tiny figures were roping stumps on the island and using the ropes to keep themselves and their horses from being washed downriver as they churned across. They might make it, he thought, but they couldn't spend much time on that island. It was nearly submerged already. And the opposite bank was steep. It was Delphine's crew. It was bound to be. They were just below the promontory where Delphine had camped, and his own crew would have headed in the opposite direction for La Partida. But why the hell hadn't they followed the herd and used the easiest and fastest crossing—the only possible crossing except for the island? Then he saw why.

One man was trying it. And from the brushy high land on the opposite bank a group of ambushers were steadily pounding bullets at him. Disregarding the flying lead, the cowboy still had all he could do to keep from being washed downstream, but he continued to churn across, ducking, dodging, floundering.

Derek's jaw set. He'd plunge in behind him, whether the cowboy made it or not. It wouldn't be the first ambush he'd ridden into. The thought had no more than entered his mind when he saw that the other rider had almost made it. His horse was pawing now at the slick ground on the opposite bank. But the man had been hit hard; he was reeling, clinging to the saddlehorn with both hands. The horse pulled himself up, and acting from blind instinct turned right and galloped into a screen of heavy brush. The rider was still hanging on somehow.

The river loomed before Derek and the stallion plunged into the icy waters. He went under and bobbed up again and Derek gasped for air. At once the first bullets splashed into the water beside him.

The current was unbelievably strong, pushing at them with the force of a watery avalanche. But Derek's dread was even stronger. A man thought more about dying—and staying alive—after he got a little older. He'd long since seen enough of death to know that there was never any glory in it, but it was worse when it came like this. It took away all dignity and showed man up for what he really was—a tiny, almost helpless creature who could get caught up in the grip

211

of the mighty elements and be destroyed as easily as an insect. But these were his cattle and he was still alive and he had a gun. And he'd known from that first day that it might come to this. And he hadn't cared.

A bullet *thucked* into the tree of his saddle. The stallion was caught sideways, spun around and swept several precious feet downstream. Derek clung to him, giving him his head. The horse recovered and angled toward the farthest point of the sloping banks. A log swept by and as Derek fended it off a slug burned its way through a fold in his soaked shirt sleeve without touching him. It brought back a feeling from that time long ago. No man wanted to be killed or wounded, but there was a special hell in your mind when you saw men on either side of you shot down and trampled—when you saw the guts of screaming horses dragging the ground, being torn out by the animals' flailing hoofs—while you rode through it all, stiff and straight, without being touched. Somehow you didn't belong to anybody or anything when it happened like that. You kept not wanting to be killed and you kept feeling guilty because you weren't. And later, when you rode out, you had a feeling that somebody was pointing a finger at you to say that you were different. Everybody worth-while had been killed back there. But not you.

A bullet splashed an inch from his knee and Derek shook the thought from his mind. One thing he had learned during that other ride into the mouths of the flaming cannon—there wasn't anything you could do but just keep heading in the direction you wanted to go. Ride straight up. If you got hit you fell; if you didn't you rode on.

The branches of a dead thorny bush swept into him and he brushed it aside. The stallion was frantically trying to keep his head above water, to shake loose from the rider, to dodge the whirling debris, to reach the other side.

Derek clung on. His legs were almost numb and his jaw set so tight his teeth ached. The fusillade grew heavier. Bullets hit the water all around him—*cannon to right of him, cannon to left of him, cannon in front of him volleyed and thundered*—

Why did he keep remembering that other time, when he'd ridden into the death-laden valley? He hadn't thought so much about living then, hadn't been so concerned about it.

Beneath the lower branches of the trees on the opposite bank he could see his herd in the distance. The stallion reached the bank and gouged upward and a bullet tore flesh from Derek's left arm. It brought a shock that coursed through his veins like swift leaden tentacles. He reined right and a feeling of gladness shot through him; he was no

213

different from anyone else. But the feeling was quickly dampened by a fear he had never experienced before. If a bullet could find his arm, another could find his body.

Lead sang about his ears as the horse raced for the cover of the brush, and then the trees were all about him. He'd gone through the valley of death once again, and somehow he was still alive.

He could see the island upriver and the tiny figures on it. Could see, too, that they were pinned there now by an expert marksman shooting down at them from the promontory where Delphine had camped last night. Every member of the crew was lying flat on muddy ground and every horse appeared to have been slain. And even in this short time the rising river had eaten farther into the banks. With no horses to help buck the current, anyone the gunman didn't kill was apt to drown.

He looked through a clearing toward the spot where the ambushers had lain in wait for him and saw Griff dart out from the brushy cover and race toward the herd.

Derek unwrapped the six-gun with stiff fingers and stuck it back in his dripping holster. If he got Griff the others would peter out soon. With no leader they'd be half-beaten already, and he'd follow along behind them for a day or two, picking off first one and then another. Before the second day had passed they'd drift away and leave the cattle and he'd get everybody from town out here again—would find another crew. And if Ridge had done his job of holding Corenson's trail herd, he might even make it. Delphine couldn't stop him next time. She'd be lucky if she had a crew left after today.

He started to swing the stallion through a gap in the brush and make a dead run for Griff. But he heard a noise in the underbrush at his feet. He whirled the black and his gun flashed into his hand. The hammer almost fell, and then he held his fire. The man at his feet was Billy Cedar.

Cedar was badly hurt. Blood stained his shirt front and had spilled onto the ground near him and his face was contorted with pain. His head was propped against a tree trunk and he was watching the island down below, flinching anew each time a bullet rang out from the mainland. His lips twisted. 'Some of Delphine's bunch are on that island.'

The gun was still in Derek's hand, barrel up. 'The hell with Delphine's bunch,' he said harshly. 'Are you badly hurt?'

Cedar shook his head, then grimaced. 'I'm an old soldier—remember? I got me some rags through them holes and I'll make out all right till the battle's over.'

'Good. I just saw Griff. I'm going after him.'

215

Cedar's eyes flashed. 'Ever'body on that island's gettin' murdered. I cain't go stop it. You got to.'

Derek shook his head and controlled the stallion. 'They're the same ones who wrecked my wagon and scattered my supplies. They're the same ones who blocked my herd last night and said pay three dollars a head or fight.'

Cedar's teeth gritted against the pain. 'Now you got a chance to show 'em what a mistake it was.'

'I've plenty of people to show.' Derek's hand tightened on the reins. 'Griff'll come first. Then I'll take care of the others.'

Cedar said bitterly, 'I sat in front of the store and heard Hees scream at you, *You don't fit in, mister*! But he was wrong, wasn't he? You fit in—just like him and Griff and Cervantes.'

'You called it wrong,' Derek gritted. 'There's only one man I want to be like now, and that's Lashner.'

'Then go on,' Cedar taunted. 'You ain't Derek Langston no more. You're Rig Lashner.' He coughed and said, 'Only you ain't. You drew on me just now and held your fire till you could see who it was. Lashner would've shot and then looked. You ain't like him.' He coughed again and his voice lowered until Derek had to strain to hear. 'I told you about Gort 'cause I didn't want you to hurt Delphine—I thought you might do somethin''

216

in one minute you'd always be sorry for. But you ain't like Gort neither. You ain't even like the Derek Langston that come over here a few weeks ago. You're just what Hees said—a plain furrin carpetbagger. And you know somethin', mister? We don't need you over here. If you cain't be like yourself, then you got nothin' to put in the pot.'

Derek watched Griff move further into the distance. He saw himself losing his herd and all he'd worked for when there was still a chance to save it. He felt a hopeless choking rising in his throat. What Cedar said was true. He'd come here and changed his clothes and put on a gun and learned how to get it out fast, and decided he was a different man. He'd figured that killing Hees had proved it, but it hadn't. No matter how much he adapted himself to the ways of this country, he still had to be Derek Langston. If he weren't, then he hadn't brought anything with him. He was only taking.

He whirled the black and looked again at the river. He wasn't plagued by guilt now; instead he felt a fear that he'd never known before. A bullet had torn flesh from him just as it had from all the others. He could be hit.

He rewrapped his six-gun, pulled on the reins, and raced upriver as far as the sloping bank would permit. The horse was tired now, and if the swift current carried them below the narrow crossing they were lost. He took a

217

swift breath, slapped the black with the ends of the reins, and plunged in.

Most of the ambushers must have followed Griff to the cattle and the two who were left must have been taken by surprise; he was halfway across before the rifles blasted out. But the first bullet slapped a hole through the stallion's right ear and the frantic, plunging horse went mad, almost got away from him. He bent low in the saddle trying to make himself a smaller target. The ridge was different this time; whatever divine providence had protected him at Balaclava and most of the way across the river the first time had suddenly turned away when the bullet had slammed into his left arm. *Ride straight up*, he had thought then. *Just keep heading in the direction you want to go.*

But now he found himself trying to urge the black to change its course as the two riflemen shot toward him with cool accuracy. He slid out of the saddle into the rushing water, clinging to a stirrup so that only his head was visible. His face was splashed and the horse screamed, and the river turned red in front of his eyes. But it was only a raking flesh wound across the stallion's shoulder. He clung on with icy fingers and tried to talk gently to the black through clamped teeth.

They hit the opposite shore and the horse scrambled and gouged its way up the bank. Derek tried to grasp the saddlehorn and vault into the saddle, but his stiff legs refused to respond.

He hung on, his boots cutting through the mud as the frenzied stallion raced across the Strip. He got an elbow up onto soaked leather and his boots slapped a stubby bush. His legs flew out behind him and he clawed his way into the saddle. He found the stirrups, swayed, and fished for the reins. He caught them and sawed hard on the jaw of the crazed animal. The black refused to stop, but Derek swung all his weight in a savage twist to the left and the horse began to change course.

They traveled in a dead run for another two hundred yards before the stallion slowed. Derek raised his eyes. Up ahead was the promontory with heavy boulders which hid the sharpshooter, who was still firing sporadically at the crew hugging the wet island below him.

Derek kept a tight rein and urged the black up the incline. The exhausted horse made it to the high ground, bowed his neck, and stopped. Derek patted the shaken animal and climbed stiffly out of the saddle. He massaged his hands, unwrapped the six-gun, and held it in front of him. A hundred yards away the tops of the boulders reared up above the brushline. He tried to picture them as he'd seen them last night, tried to figure where the gunman might be concealed. But it was no use. He'd have to move in among them and find out.

He glanced at the island but could see no change there. Unless perhaps the water were higher. His gaze swung over to the cattle, far beyond the river now and moving steadily into the distance. The faint sound of bawling animals reached his ears and he turned away. He could forget about the cattle. Crouching low he began to make his way toward the boulders, circling, trying to come up behind the sharpshooter.

His tired legs guided him into a puddle of water that splashed like a cannon shot. He stopped to listen. The boulders loomed even closer now, but he could hear no sound from that direction. Even the firing had stopped.

He moved on, reached the first giant rock, and began to skirt it. As he inched forward he watched the ground in front of him, careful not to blunder into another waterhole. A split second's advantage might mean all the difference.

The split second came when he rounded a sharp point and saw Rig Lashner facing him, grinning. Lashner's gun was also in his hand and the hammer was back and that was the edge that Derek couldn't afford.

But Lashner held his fire. 'Your hammer goes back, I shoot,' he said.

Derek wet his lips. 'I'll shoot back at least once. I promise you that.'

'There's no need for it,' Lashner said. 'I

got somethin' else in mind. I been buildin' up to it for a long time.'

'Such as?'

'You said you'd give me a hundred dollars the day you was faster'n me. There ain't nobody faster'n me, mister. There ain't never been and there ain't never goin' to be. But I give you lessons like I wouldn've done for no amount of money. I raked through my mind tryin' to think of somethin' else I might know and you didn't. An' I stood over you and saw you practice hard. An' ever' time you made a mistake I told you about it. An' this is the minute I been buildin' up to. This is why I did it all.'

Derek stood waiting, ready to flip back the hammer the instant Lashner moved.

'Now you just put it back in your holster,' Lashner said. 'An' I'll put mine back. And we'll both listen. Ever' once in a while somebody on that island down there yells. That'll be our signal. When we hear 'em yell we'll both draw.'

It was a better chance than he had now. Derek slowly began dropping the barrel of his gun and saw Lashner do the same.

The Remington slithered into wet leather and Derek's hand slid over the slick butt. The island was below his line of vision. He couldn't see the figures there, couldn't even know what the yell would sound like as it traveled through the chill damp air. He spread his fingers and tried to sharpen his hearing.

'You could draw now,' Lashner said. He grinned. 'There's no law says you got to wait on the signal. The only reason you're doin' it is 'cause you're a fool.' He shook his head wonderingly. 'You really think you're faster'n me.'

A deathly quiet settled over the promontory. *Don't think about it*, Derek warned himself. *Don't think about why you have to wait for the signal. Just listen for someone to shout*. His ears strained to pick a sound out of the hushed silence.

'Your hand ain't set right,' Lashner said. 'Your fingers are drawed up. An' you know why? 'Cause I ain't a stump, that's why. 'Cause I got a gun and I ain't scared and I'm faster'n hell, that's why.'

At the tail end of his words a shrill 'Hoooo!' sounded from the island.

Don't move sideways when you shoot!

But Derek drew with all the strength in his right arm and at the same time ducked and moved to his right. He felt the six-gun buck in his hand, felt fire rake across his neck. His own .44 slug pushed Lashner back and a second slug hammered the gunman as he triggered a wild shot. Lashner dropped to the ground, a dazed and incredulous look on his face.

The gunman's arm strained and shook as

222

he struggled to lift the gun and couldn't. After a terrible effort his hand dropped to his side and his eyes mirrored the awfulness of defeat. Blood flowed from his lips and he said weakly, 'You—you don't owe me nothin'. I shot first. I—' His teeth bit into his lip.

'Maybe you shot first,' Derek said grimly. 'But maybe I would have if I hadn't moved sideways. We'll never know.'

Lashner's teeth still clamped his lip, but Derek was talking to a dead man. A man who had built his own set of values and had never doubted their importance even as the life poured from his body.

Derek went around him and searched the brush until he found Lashner's horse. The brown stallion was only ground-tied, but still standing motionless in spite of the shooting. Derek mounted, raised his arm, and called, 'Hooo, the island! Don't shoot! I'm coming down!'

He moved into the open and down the incline, calling again, 'Langston here! You can stand now! The shooting's done!'

When they hit the Strip he urged the horse into a gallop, untying Lashner's rope and twirling it overhead. He stopped at the water's edge and made his cast, but the moment the rope left his hands he knew that it wasn't long enough. But now the others were rising from their places of concealment. He saw with a shock that Delphine was one of them, her face mud-smeared and hardly recognizable.

Beside her, Gort yelled, 'We've got ropes! You just see that they get tied to somethin'!' He shook a lariat of wet, soggy rawhide off a short stump, quickly coiled it, made a small loop, and expertly cast it over the muddy water.

Derek missed the loop, but climbed down and retrieved the lariat before the water could carry it out of reach. He found the solid root of a stunted mesquite exposed by ground that had washed away, and tied the rope to it.

'We got one dead one over here,' Gort called. 'And two that've been hit bad.'

'I'll come over and help.' Derek grasped the slick rawhide and moved into the water.

* * *

Delphine Judson was the last to be brought back across. The cold waters cleansed the mud from her face, and as she pulled herself up to the level of the shoreline Derek looked into her eyes for any hint of softness or welcome and found none.

'You win,' she said. 'I'll have to help you now. You saved the Otis kid, and the people in town had to help. And now you've saved me and I have to help.'

'I didn't even know you were on the island,' Derek said.

224

She came clear out of the water and stood near him, dripping wet. Her eyes narrowed. 'Then why did you come back? Was it because you thought my crew would help you?'

'I came back because of the old man Gort went after a few minutes ago,' Derek said. 'Because of Billy Cedar. He made me see something that I'd lost sight of. If he'd been dead, or if he'd just have kept his mouth shut I could have saved my herd. But I'm not sorry the cattle are gone. And I'll get them back whether I have your help or not.'

'We were going to scatter your cattle and run you out of the country,' Delphine said woodenly. 'We still would if things hadn't turned out this way.'

'I was strong enough to give up the cattle,' Derek said. 'And I'm strong enough to keep you from taking them. You or anyone else!'

Delphine's eyes were uncertain, but she said stubbornly, 'You must have known I was there. Or you must have been banking on help from my crew.'

Derek shook his head pityingly. 'If I'd known you were there it would have been enough to bring me back,' he admitted. 'But I didn't know it. I didn't have time to think about it. I came back simply because there were people on the island and they were in trouble. But you can believe what you like! I have something better to do than stand here.'

He mounted Lashner's horse and looked back down at her. Her eyes were filled with tears and it startled him. She turned away to stifle the sobs and he shook his head in wonderment. Looking back on it now, it seemed a little thing, a natural thing, to help someone out of trouble whether you knew them or not. And because it was such a natural thing, it hardly seemed likely that this was the reason Delphine was crying. Perhaps she was only exhausted from the ordeal on the island.

He turned the horse; there was no time to puzzle it out today. There were dead to be buried and wounded to patch up, supplies to be gotten, a crew to be found, and preparations to be made for tomorrow.

He touched his spurs to the stallion's ribs. First of all he'd see if he could do anything for Billy Cedar.

CHAPTER EIGHTEEN

Derek stood in the doorway of the Judson ranch bunkhouse and marveled at the warm March sun still only minutes above the horizon but already giving hints of the balmy day to come. It was almost unbelievable that yesterday the whole countryside had been drenched with a torrential chilling rain.

The yard was bustling with activity. Dogs raced back and forth barking with excitement as the Judson cowhands chec ked their gear against the rigors of the coming chase. Billy Cedar was an old soldier, all right. Wounded and tired, he'd nevertheless directed all the preparations. Only now, when all was in order, had he consented to rest. The crew had been hot to follow Griff immediately, but Cedar had been adamant. 'The trail'll be as easy to foller tomorrow, and they cain't move fast with that herd. We need dry guns, and we need grub and ammunition. First thing in the mornin's soon enough!'

He'd been right, of course. Half the six-guns in the outfit wouldn't have fired at all and only four rifles had clean barrels. And if that hadn't been reason enough to delay, the arrival during the night of Jackson and three of Derek's trail hands would have been. 'It was ol' Otis,' Jackson explained sheepishly. 'When we went by the ranch house he like to've gone out of his mind. Tried to get Sary to help him into that ol' buggy. Had a fool idea he was better'n nothin'. Would've come, too, if we hadn't promised to turn around.'

'Thanks,' Derek had said. 'I'm glad to have you back.'

And this morning Grayson and four other men from town had arrived. This time they had not come expecting a picnic. They were cool and businesslike and steady. 'We had a

227

meetin' last night,' Grayson said grimly, 'and I got elected sheriff. It's high time we all had some protection around here!'

Derek saw Adelita come to the door of the ranch house and wondered about Delphine. After they'd brought Billy Cedar across the river yesterday she'd spoken to him alone and then had broken into uncontrollable sobs that shook her body and refused to stop. She was still crying when she'd mounted her blue roan and raced for the ranch. He'd tried to catch up with her to talk, but it was no use, and by the time he'd reached the house Adelita was shooing all the men away. They hadn't seen her since.

Adelita came toward him now and her broad Indian face seemed almost to smile. 'La patrona wishes to see you, please.'

Derek fell in behind her and as they skirted the busy men Adelita said, 'Since before the war we have not had so many visitors here.'

He looked at her curiously, 'Have you been with the Judsons long?'

'Very long. Since Delphine was born.' She turned and put a hand on his arm to stop him. 'She has had much trouble, señor. You—will be kind, no?' She looked at the bulge caused by the bandage beneath his shirt sleeve. 'And, señor—I hope your arm is well—soon.' She went past him quickly and entered the house.

Derek paused in the doorway. Delphine's

back was to him and she was staring into the fire, her hands crammed into the pockets of her brush jacket. She turned toward him and he was startled at the softness he saw in her face.

'I'm sorry—about everything,' she said.

He walked over to her. 'I'm still the same man I was,' he reminded. 'And I still own the Strip.'

She nodded and her eyes grew moist. 'I—I didn't think there was anyone left who would risk his life just for—just for—people.'

'You haven't taken stock for a long time,' Derek said softly. 'There's Billy Cedar and Sam Otis and Dan Grayson—and Gort almost went out of his mind yesterday when Adelita wouldn't let him come in to see how you really were.'

'I know. And you—will you forgive me?'

He put his hands on either side of her face and drew it close. 'There's nothing to forgive. We all have yesterdays we'd rather forget.'

He bent and kissed her, and then was annoyed because Grayson called from outside, 'Langston! We're waitin' on you!'

They drew apart, and he said exultantly, 'We'll have the biggest ranch around here—and we'll raise the biggest, fattest cattle!'

She laughed tremulously. 'At a time like this, some people think about raising children.'

He laughed. 'When we get back I'll make it a real proposal and then we'll talk about all of it.' He kissed her quickly and started for the door, waiting while she picked up her hat and pushed her hair up into it. They were smiling as they went out into the yard.

Gort called, 'You all right, Miss Delphine?'

She mounted the roan. 'Yes, Gort. I'm fine, thanks.'

'Okay, men,' Grayson yelled. 'Let's go!'

The dun was facing south and as Derek swung into the saddle, he saw three riders approach. 'Hold it a minute, Grayson! Here come three more men. And two of them are wearing blue uniforms!'

Gort whirled his horse, looked and whistled between his teeth. 'Well, if that don't beat hell! An' you know somethin', mister? That third 'un used to be a Texas Ranger 'fore they did away with the Rangers. There ain't no tellin' what'll come along next!'

A babble of conversation rose up, but snipped off as the three men rode into the ranch yard.

Delphine reined over toward them. The ex-Ranger tipped his hat. 'Ma'am. Name's Sam Claybourne. This here's Sergeant Kirby and Corporal Dobbs. Over to the Fort we heard about a killin' that happened last Sunday.'

The men were gathering around in a tight circle now and both soldiers looked wary.

'Then I'm the one you want to see,' Derek said. 'It was I who killed Casper Hees.'

'We don't care about that,' Claybourne said. 'From what we heard, he needed killin'. But somebody wired his nephew from the Fort, and the nephew wired back that we'd find a bounty-jumper—a deserter—out here some place. A feller named Griff. These two Yankee soldiers want to pick him up.'

Gort chimed in, 'You helpin' Yankee soldiers these days? Is that why you come along?'

The ex-Ranger pushed his hat back and scratched his head, shifting uncomfortably in the saddle. 'Well, no, not exactly,' he drawled. 'I'm just servin' as a guide. Jobs ain't too easy to get these days, and seein' they was only after a Yankee anyway, I figgered it wouldn't hurt if I helped 'em a little.'

Gort cackled. 'Well if that just don't beat hell! Where'd you fight, Yankee boy?'

Sergeant Kirby bristled. 'If you was in the same fight, Johnny, you done the runnin'!'

Gort turned beet red and shut up as the men around him laughed.

'That deserter you mentioned,' Derek said. 'He and a good-sized crew have got my cattle. We're going after them.'

Claybourne turned toward Sergeant Kirby. 'What do you think, Yankee?'

'Suits me,' Kirby said promptly. 'We'll go.'

231

Grayson waved his arm. 'Then let's get started.' He led off and the others began to fall in behind him in pairs. Derek rode beside Delphine, and Gort, after shooing the dogs back, cut in front of them and moved up beside Grayson.

'You think Langston'll start his drive as soon as we get back?' Derek heard Grayson ask.

'Naw,' Gort said. 'Miss Delphine has already sent ol' Corenson five hundred dollars so he can hold out till we can join up with 'im. 'Tween all of us, we'll make the damnedest drive that was ever made.' He chuckled. 'You wouldn't take that Langston for a feller that'd tell tall tales, now would you? But you know, he told me he wouldn't ever leave this country 'cause it had been in his family for eight hundred years. And damned if I don't halfway believe him the way he took to it.'

Grayson laughed shortly but his shoulders still bent in dejection.

'You worried about this fight we're goin' to?' Gort asked.

Grayson nodded. 'Some.'

'Well, then,' Gort said. 'You look at it this way. We got us an ex-Texas Ranger and two Yankee boys, eleven men who wore Confed'rate gray, and one Englishman who rode in the charge of the Light Brigade. The way I see it, we'll be back in maybe five, six

232

days, and we'll have the cattle with us.'

Grayson's shoulders straightened and Derek grinned. That about summed it up, he thought. Except for one thing. This time he'd make that first forty miles.

Photoset, printed and bound in Great Britain by REDWOOD PRESS LIMITED, Melksham, Wiltshire